P/12

Delta County Libraries

PO BOX 858
Delta, CO 81416
www.deltalibraries.org

DANGER IN THE DARK

A HOUDINI & NATE MYSTERY

TOM LALICKI

Pictures by **Carlyn Cerniglia**

SQUARE
FISH

FARRAR, STRAUS AND GIROUX
NEW YORK

For Barbara, again and always

SQUARE
FISH

An Imprint of Macmillan

DANGER IN THE DARK. Text copyright © 2006 by Tom Lalicki.
Pictures copyright © 2006 by Carlyn Cerniglia. All rights reserved.
Distributed in Canada by H.B. Fenn and Company Ltd.
Printed in March 2010 in the United States of America
by R. R. Donnelley & Sons Company, Harrisonburg, Virginia.
For information, address Square Fish, 175 Fifth Avenue,
New York, NY 10010.

Square Fish and the Square Fish logo are trademarks of Macmillan
and are used by Farrar, Straus and Giroux under license from Macmillan.

Library of Congress Cataloging-in-Publication Data
Lalicki, Tom.
    Danger in the dark : a Houdini & Nate mystery / Tom Lalicki.
       p.   cm.
    Summary: Thirteen-year-old Nathaniel, aided by the famous
magician Harry Houdini, plots to unmask a phony spirit adviser
attempting to relieve the boy's great-aunt of her fortune.
    ISBN: 978-0-312-60214-7
    1. Houdini, Harry, 1874–1926—Juvenile fiction. [1. Houdini,
Harry, 1874–1926—Fiction.   2. Magicians—Fiction.
3. Spiritualists—Fiction.]   I. Title.

PZ7.L1594Dan 2006
[Fic]—dc22

2005052111

Originally published in the United States by Farrar, Straus and Giroux
Square Fish logo designed by Filomena Tuosto
Designed by Jay Colvin
First Square Fish Edition: 2010
10 9 8 7 6 5 4 3 2 1
www.squarefishbooks.com

DANGER IN THE DARK

I keep six honest serving men
  (They taught me all I knew)
Their names are What and Where and When
And How and Why and Who.
                    —Rudyard Kipling

Prologue

The voices, the strange, anguished voices, woke him from a deep sleep the first time it happened. And the second time, too.

Both nights he stayed under the covers and tried to figure out what was going on downstairs. Who were these frenzied people in the parlor? Surely not his mother and aunt. Who?

The boy stayed awake as late as possible after that, waiting for the next time. On his fifth night's watch, he heard the telltale sounds. He crept from his bed to the hallway and crouched at the top of the stairs to listen.

The voices bleeding through the French doors were more distinct but still made no sense. A man with a deep voice and a strange accent—maybe an Indian—spoke most often. At other times different women talked, but they practically yelled, as if trying to be heard by someone far away. Once, he was certain that Aunt Alice was speaking.

Suddenly the man's voice changed. The accent was gone, the pitch was higher. It was Mr. Trane speaking, of course.

David Douglas Trane was his aunt's new friend. Mr. Trane was the only man he could ever remember visiting her in the evening. The spooky, late-night gatherings started the week his aunt met Mr. Trane.

The boy eavesdropped from the landing half a dozen times but felt he was no closer to understanding. And he sensed that no one wanted him to understand.

Overcome by curiosity one night, he crawled to his mother's door and cracked it open to reveal an empty bed in a darkened room. His mother was downstairs. She was a member of the party even though he never once heard her speak.

And she never once breathed a word of the goings-on to him, not in two months. He tried to keep his imagination in check but could not understand what secrets she was keeping, or why.

The school year ends soon, he thought. *That will change things.* When the family went to Connecticut for the summer, everything would return to normal. Surely Mr. Trane would not go to the country with them. *Would he?*

1

Nathaniel G. Makeworthy Fuller was almost thirteen, but far too slight to shoulder a name as weighty as his. Dissatisfied with his answer to a question, any teacher could stretch *Nath-an-i-el* or *Na-than-iel* into a powerful rebuke. And schoolmates never tired of speculating what he was made worthy of or if he was worth anything at all.

Complaining did no good. "Yours is a name to be proud of, young man—a name to be reckoned with, indeed" was his aunt Alice's mechanical reply. But her voice was not mechanical in the dreary way an ice-wagon horse clip-clopped down the street or the listless way a fruit vendor yelled out "Strawberries!" or a tinker cried "Pots and pans! I'll mend your pots and pans!" No, Aunt Alice's favorite sayings always sounded exactly the same, as if she was thinking it and saying it for the first time, the way a player-piano roll always repeats a tune. Frightening, really. The only consolation Nathaniel's mother ever offered was a hushed "At least you don't have to use 'the Fourth.'" Hushed because Aunt Alice naturally assumed that he announced himself to the world as Nathaniel G. Makeworthy Fuller IV.

So it was an unexpected joy to find himself being called simply Mr. Fuller for the last two days. Of course, everybody who worked at Bennett & Son, Gentlemen's Hatters of Fifth Avenue near Thirteenth Street, was called "Mr."—from the impossibly old, white-haired Mr. Bennett, who came every afternoon at four to take tea in the inner office with his son (also Mr. Bennett, also white-haired), right down to Nathaniel, the least experienced clerk's assistant.

According to Mr. Winchell, the fifteen-year-old junior clerk Nathaniel assisted, Mr. Fuller should think of himself as a "dogsbody." Before he could ask, Nathaniel was told that a dogsbody was a worthless drudge, a menial nobody, a slave who did everything his master said or else he would find out what.

Clearly the advantages of being treated as an adult did not outweigh the disadvantages. All of Nathaniel's previous summers—all that he could remember—had been frittered away at his aunt's lake house in Connecticut. Nathaniel had summer friends there, friends who were probably lolling on front porches, lazy from the sun's heat, trying to decide what to do next this beautiful afternoon.

As a working man—a dogsbody—in this summer of 1911, Nathaniel had no such concerns. Mr. Winchell filled Nathaniel's day with work. From eight-thirty, when he donned a heavy canvas apron and swept the street in front of Bennett's, to half past five in the evening, when they locked the doors, Nathaniel labored. Mr. Winchell, who was only two years older, must have shaken his head in disgust ten times that day and once told Nathaniel, "I can't stand the sight of a lazy boy standing about being lazy."

Winchell kept him far too busy to dwell on the topsy-turvy developments that had forced the family to remain in New York for the summer and made Nathaniel, unexpectedly, a working man.

"Young man, this should not be a problem!" boomed a voice from across the floor. A customer was speaking to Mr. Winchell. "It is no problem, is it?" the man asked very forcefully.

"No, sir, it is not, sir," said Mr. Winchell. "But it *is*, sir, since Mr. Bennett has just left with our senior clerk to show hat styles to a member of the Serbian royal family, a prince, sir, who is visiting New York and staying at the Hotel Brevoort a few blocks down, and so while I am the senior staff member on duty, since you do not have an account with us presently and have, sir, as you have said, no identification, I feel that I cannot open an account for you, sir."

As the words tumbled from Mr. Winchell, Nathaniel took several silent half steps to his right, gaining a sight line to the customer. And what a striking sight he was. Slightly shorter than Mr. Winchell, the customer seemed like a circus strongman in a checked suit. Nathaniel had never seen any man whose arm muscles and chest pressed out from his clothes. Important men—presidents, mayors, ministers—had huge stomachs that pushed out a foot or more ahead as they walked. This customer's waist slanted in. And even standing twenty paces away, Nathaniel saw bright blue-gray eyes set in the customer's square, muscular face. A new Bennett & Son derby topped his thick, black-coiled hair but could not contain it all; wiry hair curled around the hat's brim. Nathaniel thought that the customer was struggling to keep back a smile.

"If the gentleman could supply us with references? We have a telephone, we could call," said Mr. Winchell.

"Ha," said the customer as he flicked a glance to his right, then instantly turned and bent slightly to his left and suddenly had a white terrier in his arms. Nathaniel shuddered, unable to tell whether the customer had bent to pick up the dog or the dog had leapt into his arms or they had simultaneously met in the middle.

"I fear," the customer continued, "that you will find my dog Charlie less than a one hundred percent reference. I have sterling human references—alas, not Serbian princes. But my references *may* be difficult to reach by phone. Although I understand that Mr. Bell and his workmen are, at this very minute, running telephone wires from New York to Chicago. Someday we might be able to call all the way to San Francisco. But that's neither here nor there, is it, young man?"

Nathaniel was certain now that the customer was smiling.

"Let's see . . . There is Sergei, the Grand Duke of Russia. The Imperial Chief of Police in Berlin. Of course, the Chief Constable of Scotland Yard, who is a very good friend of Mr. Sherlock Holmes as well. Don't you feel *any* of those worthy gentlemen would do?"

Gotcha, Nathaniel thought, pleased with himself. *Sherlock Holmes isn't a real person. He's only in books. This man is putting one over on Mr. Winchell.* Nathaniel realized that he must be smiling himself because the customer winked at him. Or did he really?

"Those are fine people, sir, but isn't there anyone here in New York we could contact?" Mr. Winchell's voice strained; he wasn't in on the joke yet.

"I do not spend very much time in this fair city, my dear sir. I happen to know that several of my revered colleagues—including Ching Ling Soo and Progea the Wildman—are only blocks away at Tony Pastor's Theater on Fourteenth Street. But they are probably engaged in a performance at the moment."

Mr. Winchell was speechless, obviously confused. Maybe embarrassed.

"This is entirely my fault, young sir," the customer said,

as if transformed. "I often leave the house forgetting everything but Charlie. Some days I walk miles because I lack the nickel for a trolley or an El train." The customer patted about his coat and trouser pockets.

"Let me confide this to you. My wife, adorable in every way, will be *severely* disappointed if I return home without a new hat—she gave my last to a passing hack driver's horse, claiming that it was *zu lumpig*! Aah, you don't speak German . . . 'too shabby' she called my hat.

"There!" the customer exclaimed as he drew a calling card from an inside coat pocket and placed it on the counter. "Will wonders never cease?"

Depositing the dog Charlie also on a glass countertop, the customer fished a pencil stub from his pocket and wrote on the back of his calling card, then reached around the taller Mr. Winchell's shoulders and pulled him close.

"Our plan is this: I shall wear this fine new hat home and will unquestionably purchase more hats; Bennett & Son will be my New York hatter. You shall present my card to your employer, who will establish an account for me and post a statement in the mail to that address—my New York home quarters—and I shall settle the debt promptly. Agreed?"

But before the trembling junior clerk could agree or disagree, the customer, his dog, and the unpaid-for hat were through the door and moving north on Fifth Avenue.

"What will Mr. Bennett say?" Nathaniel asked. Mr. Winchell groaned.

2

Recognizing him instantly, by sight, to be a gentleman of quality . . ."

Mr. Winchell was explaining the situation later that morning to young Mr. Bennett.

"Quality?" interrupted Mr. Simpson, the store's senior clerk. "*I've* read, in the *World*, I believe, that he's a gypsy, an immigrant from Romania or Austria-Hungary."

"Yes, Mr. Simpson, I'm sure. I believe I've read—in the *Times*—that he's from Wisconsin," said the young Mr. Bennett quite sharply. "Please, allow your junior clerk to continue."

Nathaniel stood nearby, dusting hat samples he had

already dusted. He was keen to hear Mr. Winchell spin more of this fabulously made-up story.

"Well then," struggled Mr. Winchell, "recognizing him instantly to be a person of great importance . . ."

As a word took shape in Mr. Simpson's mouth, Mr. Bennett shot the senior clerk a withering glance.

". . . I suggested that the gentleman take his hat straightaway and that we would open an account and bill him presently. Of course, I suggested that he might want a second hat—a suggestion to which he agreed."

"Very quick-witted, very professional," Mr. Bennett said rather flatly. Still looking at Mr. Winchell, he said, "Young Mr. Fuller. I take it that you observed this exceptional interview. Did you learn from it?"

"Yes," said Nathaniel meekly, wanting to say he had learned that Mr. Winchell was a very quick-witted liar.

"What did you learn, young man?" asked Mr. Bennett in a rising tone that told Nathaniel he needed to be quick-witted himself.

"I learned that the customer is always right, sir."

"Indeed!" boomed Mr. Bennett in a very ominous voice Nathaniel had not heard before. "The *customer* is always right! But the *stranger* walking in off the avenue is not. He is not a customer unless he makes a purchase and pays for it."

Trying desperately to redeem himself, Mr. Winchell blurted, "But we examined his calling card, sir. We both did—Fuller and myself."

"The correct form grammatically is 'Fuller and I,' " interjected Mr. Simpson. "But you should always address—"

"The calling card *is* impressive," Mr. Bennett said as he reexamined it.

And it certainly had impressed Nathaniel and Mr. Winchell after the gentleman bolted.

The card proclaimed, in very stylish lettering:

HOUDINI
*The World's Handcuff King and **Only** Prison Breaker*
Known in Every Country Around the World

Mr. Winchell was one up on Nathaniel, because he seemed to be very well acquainted with Mr. Houdini's doings. Nathaniel had heard of him but thought that Harry Houdini was like Sherlock Holmes—a character from books.

"Impressive, but possibly completely false," continued Mr. Bennett. "The *real* Houdini himself has warned that the streets are honeycombed with coat thieves, purse thieves, umbrella thieves. There are supposedly enough hat thieves to form a human bridge across the Hudson River to Hoboken. And the real Houdini has said that one of their tricks is using false calling cards. A lengthy interview in the *Times* revealed that information." He said this last bit directly to Mr. Simpson.

"Mr. Winchell, did it never occur to you how irregular

it is for a *real* gentleman to travel without a billfold? To be abroad without a hat?"

"He was an irregular gentleman," Mr. Winchell said in his own defense.

"Mr. Winchell, you will now make this situation regular," Mr. Bennett said sternly. "You will go to the address scrawled on the back of this card, present a bill for eight dollars, and return with the payment. Otherwise, you will have that eight dollars deducted from your earnings at a rate of fifty cents weekly. Now, back to our regular occupations." With that, Mr. Bennett swiftly retired to his office.

Mr. Winchell had Miss O'Reilly, the bookkeeper, type a bill for "Mr. Houdini, 278 West 113th Street, New York, payable on demand." He folded the paper and slipped it into an envelope. When they were alone on the floor, he thrust it at Nathaniel.

"This is *all* your fault, you little rich boy," he seethed. "You should have said something when that impostor was bullying me. You should have gone for help. You should have blocked the door to keep him in."

Nathaniel cringed but remained silent.

"This is *not* going to cost me," Mr. Winchell continued, more calm but very grave. "Mine is the only paycheck my mother and sisters have. Fifty cents a week to us is sugar for coffee and cake. And I like sugar in my coffee and I like my mother's cakes. If you don't collect that eight dollars, I'll take it out of you."

"Me?"

"You, Mr. Fuller. Go to Harlem and get Houdini to pay that bill."

"But—"

"Understand me!" Mr. Winchell said menacingly. "Leave the store now and return before closing with the money. How you do it isn't any business of mine, rich boy."

Nathaniel was torn. No, he was caught in the horns of a dilemma, as his Sunday Bible Study teacher liked to say. The expression always made him wonder: What sort of animal was a dilemma? And what sort of horns did it have — giant, curved ones with lots of sharp points, like the elk and moose President Roosevelt hunted out west? Or did a dilemma just have stubby little horns, like a nanny goat?

Now he decided the horns were big and sharp.

One part of him hoped that Mr. Houdini lived at the address typed on the envelope; another part hoped that he did not. Thinking *Heads I lose, tails I lose*, Nathaniel realized that he finally understood what a dilemma is. If Mr. Houdini was home, he had to collect eight dollars from a man who might not want to pay or might want to bargain over the price. A man who could talk circles around anybody.

The alternative was no better. If the man who had left Bennett & Son with a brushed-felt derby hat was not really Mr. Houdini, Nathaniel had to find eight dollars for Mr. Winchell to put in the cash drawer.

He thought fleetingly of telling Mr. Winchell the money was *his* responsibility but flatly rejected that path. Mr. Winchell had a deep streak of New York tough. Who could better spot a tough than a toff? Nathaniel had been called a toff and worse—snob, swell, pantywaist—often enough to recognize a threat. Mr. Winchell was no street arab; he was not a homeless orphan with a knife who would slit your throat for a price. He probably knew a few who would, though. There were thousands of homeless urchins on New York City's streets to be feared.

"Rich boy." That echoed in his head. *Is it so obvious?* Nathaniel asked himself. He understood why he was regularly taunted on the way to and from school. In his St. Paul's Day School blazer and tie, he stood out from boys going to public school. He stood out even more from boys his age who did not attend school at all. Many worked all day, even though every child under fourteen was supposed to be in school.

His family—that is, Nathaniel, his mother, and his great-aunt Alice—lived in a town house. And there was Jennie, the live-in housekeeper, as well. Four floors for four people. He knew that he was rich, but he did not feel rich.

The only time he ever had money to spend on something he wanted was their once-a-year visit to Dreamland Park at Coney Island, Brooklyn's seaside resort. Aunt Alice reluctantly approved of Dreamland Park because it was built by a notable Christian businessman and had so much educational content. Aunt Alice assumed they visited and revisited the Creation Building, which took visitors through the story of Genesis. The next stop should have been the Japanese Teahouse and then Tour of the Alps. They did all that once, then Nathaniel's mother said, "Once is enough." His mother always gave him some pocket money to spend, and spend he did. Nathaniel roared through the water on Shoot the Chutes, explored Africa and Hades through the tunnels of the Dragon's Gorge, saw the wild tigers of Bostock's Circus.

But every time it quickly came down to a choice: *Should I spend this on another ride on the Shoot the Chutes or buy cotton candy? Or treat Mother to a ride down the Helter Skelter, the water ride for ladies?*

All these thoughts bounced around his head, as if jarred loose by the rolling motion and the frightful screeches of the subway train he was riding uptown. In 1904, the Interborough Rapid Transit Company had opened its Broadway subway line all the way to 145th Street. He had walked from Bennett & Son to the Fourteenth Street station, paid a nickel fare from the emergency reserve his mother had given him, and boarded an uptown train. The ride was close and dark between stations; many people defiantly said they would never ride underground—that was for miners. Riding the subway was less interesting than riding the elevated trains, which let you catch glimpses into people's windows. It was less interesting than riding the electric trolleys, which careened up and down the avenues at frightening speeds, terrifying both pedestrians and horses. But if you were going all the way from Fourteenth Street to 113th Street, the subway was surely the fastest route.

After exiting the subway at the 110th Street station and walking north a few blocks, Nathaniel decided that if Mr. Houdini lived here, he could certainly afford a hat. West 113th Street, filled with solid brick homes, looked much like East Fifty-third Street, where Nathaniel lived. The thought of home brought David Douglas Trane to mind, unfortunately. Before Trane's arrival, Nathaniel never thought about how things were at home. Now the house was filled with late-night comings and goings. The air was thick with tension and secrets.

Nathaniel wondered if Mr. Houdini's house would be as odd as its owner. But number 278 looked ordinary. Ordinary, that is, for a house having its handsome front partly knocked down. Workmen were shrouded by a cloud of stone dust as their hammers and chisels opened up a gaping hole in the wall of the house's ground floor. On the stone stairs, above the cloud, stood a tiny woman—much shorter than Nathaniel's mother—who shouted to the workmen below in a voice much larger than Nathaniel's mother's: "Don't make the opening too large . . . Don't go any further than Houdini's plans show . . . You have looked at Houdini's plans, yes? . . . And you have measured?"

"Yes," one of the workers grunted repeatedly.

"Oh, where is Houdini when you *need* him?"

This lady knows Houdini. Seizing his chance, Nathaniel rushed the stairs and blurted out his story.

"Mr. Houdini bought a hat today at Bennett & Son, ma'am, and forgot to pay for it. I'm here to ask him, uh, well, I was sent to collect the account—eight dollars, that is—for the hat."

Turning and looking downward, the tiny lady shook her head, saying *"Das war dumm,"* or something like that. Something Nathaniel certainly did not understand.

"I said, 'That was a silly thing to do'—referring to my husband. But it is silly of me to think you speak German . . . since you spoke to me in English . . . Silly, silly, silly."

As she spoke, she walked down the stairs, reached her arm around Nathaniel's neck. She was giddy, aflutter.

"My mother and Houdini's mother speak only German. At home in New York, we speak German. But now, young man," she said with a forced seriousness, "you told me that Houdini bought a hat he did not pay for. If you will kindly come inside and share a piece of cake with me, I will not speak any more German to you and we will settle this matter. Agreed?"

The tiny lady was strong. She practically pulled Nathaniel up the stairs at double speed, so quickly he nearly missed the sign saying LEOPOLD WEISS, M.D., in the first-floor window. As they entered the narrow hallway, he noticed that the first door on the right was closed and had a DOCTOR'S OFFICE sign. To the left was an open parlor. A waiting room? Maybe this was a boardinghouse, and the little lady, who had let loose her grip and was walking ahead, was the landlady.

"Let me read your mind," she said, turning to Nathaniel, "since my husband and I are expert in that field. That is my brother-in-law's office. He is right now consulting on an experimental brain surgery. We are so very proud. Leo is a specialist in X-rays. Do you know what X-rays are, young man?"

"No . . . maybe. I'm not sure."

"*Natürlich*, why should you? But they are very important. Doctors use X-rays—they are invisible, you know— to see inside your body, to see if you have a broken bone or if you have a growth on your brain. And would you believe it was a French *woman* doctor who invented them?"

She paused, but before Nathaniel realized he was expected to say something, the lady started up again.

"As I think about it, maybe she did not invent X-rays, she probably discovered them. She *found* these invisible rays and somehow locked them in a giant metal box? I'm not sure; you should ask Houdini."

"Is Mr. Houdini here?"

"No 'Mr.' is necessary, young man. 'Houdini is enough,' as he likes to say. And he may be here, but I do not think he is. Let's go to the kitchen, where it is quiet."

At the end of the hallway, the lady opened a door, and Nathaniel followed her into . . . the kitchen? There was a stove, a sink, a refrigerator, two large metal boxes the size of refrigerators, and, at the back windows, a cage filled with birds.

But not like any birdcage Nathaniel had ever seen. He judged this one wide enough to house a circus lion and tall enough for a circus bear to stand up in. Inside it were ledges, perches, branches, swings, and what looked like dozens of birds. Unconsciously, Nathaniel had walked up to the cage and put his hands against the rigid wire, with electrifying results. One startled bird squawked and took flight, then another and another, until they were all screeching and dithering in bird panic. The lady rushed to his side, singing sweetly to the birds in a foreign language—it must have been more German—until they all settled back down onto perches or clung to the wire and stared at Nathaniel with distrust.

"Sit, please sit at the table, young man," she said. "Many people come in here, and I never remember to warn them. The birds are all so beautiful; is this why they are all so easily frightened? But, a young businessman like you has no time for Mrs. Houdini's feathered children, does he?"

She was having fun with him, he was positive. But not making fun of him. She was very different from Aunt Alice and his teachers, who were so stern, always stern. And his mother was mostly sad, too sad for fun. But Mrs. Houdini, she seemed to twinkle. She was happy, like a tiny moving smile, flitting about.

"So Houdini left your store with a hat? Is it a *fine* hat?"

That jerked Nathaniel back. The bill, the store, and Mr. Winchell rushed into his mind. "Yes, ma'am, a very fine derby hat. That's the only kind Bennett & Son sells, ma'am," he added mechanically.

"Wonderful. He should have bought five hats, ten! My husband"—she leaned toward him—"is first-rate and top-notch in everything but his *wardrobe*. Left on his own, the man would wear the same clothes until they turned to rags. And when the tatters fell off his back, Houdini would pay no attention and walk the streets stark naked. *Das ist die reine Wahrheit!*"

At the word *naked*, Nathaniel choked on the delicious cakelike bread Mrs. Houdini had served him.

"Forgive me again," she said. "I promised no more German and failed. I meant, 'That is the absolute truth.' Is that what bothered you?"

Nathaniel hesitated a long second and then blurted out the truth. "No, ma'am. It was your language, ma'am."

"My language? . . . My language? I do not understand. Houdini and I have spent countless nights refining our native speech . . . suppressing our *dems* and *dose* . . . learning the 'King's English.' And we have spoken before kings. So what is wrong with my language?"

Looking away from the aroused woman, Nathaniel meekly said, "It's just that I've never heard a lady talk about a man being *na*—, being without clothes."

Sure, boys in school said that, and worse, all the time.

But only quietly, when they knew no teachers could hear.

It seemed to be a long, long time before Mrs. Houdini asked, "How old are you, my young man?"

"Thirteen, ma'am, in a few months."

"And you have never heard the word *naked* used in the school yard? Or in your Sunday school? You've never heard of Noah's nakedness?"

"Yes, ma'am, but Noah was punished for it, too, wasn't he?"

Laughter bubbled up in Mrs. Houdini and spilled out. "Indeed, he was."

She jumped up and scurried out the doorway, her voice trailing off as she said, "Will it shock you to know that you have just sold a very fine derby hat to the world's most famous naked man? A Bennett & Son hat!"

Alone in the kitchen, Nathaniel just listened to the dozens of birds chirping and cooing and tapping behind him.

3

Mrs. Houdini charged back into the room carrying a thick leather folder nearly half as big as she was herself. And talking as fast as she moved, she appeared to finish the thought she had started earlier.

"On second thought, Adam is a more famous naked man than Houdini, but Houdini is still young."

As she opened the huge folder, Nathaniel could see that it was a memorabilia album. The first page she showed Nathaniel had a theatrical poster. In the center of the poster was a picture of the man in question. The wording proclaimed: THE TREMENDOUS SUCCESS OF HOUDINI, THE SENSATION OF LONDON. Another poster declared: HARRY HOUDINI—THE

WORLD'S GREATEST MYSTIFIER. She showed him pages with newspaper stories: HOUDINI'S IMPOSSIBLE ESCAPE and HOUDINI TRIUMPHS AGAIN. She flipped to a page with pictures of Houdini in what Nathaniel called opera clothes: a white bow tie, high white collar, and shiny black suit. But Houdini was also wearing handcuffs, leg-irons, and chains.

Nathaniel laughed suddenly.

"My aunt Alice has a friend, a 'spirit adviser' she calls him, who dresses like that. Imagining *him* in chains is funny."

"A spiritual adviser," she asked, "or a spirit adviser? These are not the same thing."

"I'm not sure," Nathaniel said, aware that he was telling a complete lie to a very nice person because he was . . . embarrassed to admit the truth? Afraid? "It doesn't matter, ma'am."

"If you say so, then it does not matter," she said, turning the page. And bingo, Houdini was naked.

Staring straight out, Houdini stood in a stooped position. His arms and legs were in irons and connected by chains so short that he was forced to bend at the waist. An iron collar was around his neck. A thick chain connected that iron to the others. All the chains were held together by giant padlocks. His body was turned at an angle, and his manacled arms covered the middle of his body so it appeared that Houdini was completely unclothed.

Nathaniel's eye moved to the facing picture, where

Houdini was standing in a jail cell. He seemed to be pulling the cell door open as he dangled a mass of chains and body irons in his free hand. In this picture, Houdini was wearing some clothes, if you could call a white cloth that looked like a baby's diaper "clothes."

"People may be shocked by what Houdini does, but they love to see him do it," Mrs. Houdini said. "Young man, I think you have surely seen some of these stories in the newspapers?"

"I don't read newspapers much, ma'am." *"Much" is an exaggeration.* "My aunt Alice hasn't allowed a newspaper in the house for a very long time. Since before I could read," he said.

"But you go to school, yes? You must pass newsstands. This summer you work on Fifth Avenue. I wager that every man you work with reads a newspaper, am I right? And you have no curiosity?"

Stunned, Nathaniel tried to find some excuse: "Well, I guess I've just never been interested." Unwillingly he conjured up the image of his aunt Alice as a heavy woolen blanket, covering him, smothering both him and his mother. His mother was just as afraid of her as he was. No, his mother must be more frightened of Aunt Alice than he was.

"A boy your age not interested in the baseball, or when the circus comes to town?"

"My aunt Alice has not allowed a newspaper in her house since my father died," he blurted. "It was in all the newspapers, and it made her . . . very angry, I guess. So my mother always told me never to look at newspapers because I might accidentally talk about something I had read and get my aunt angry again."

Mrs. Houdini sighed very deeply. She slumped into a chair at the table's corner and stared for a while. Turning to Nathaniel, she asked, "But how would she know what is in the papers if she does not read them?"

"I never thought of that."

Mrs. Houdini smiled again.

"We must attend to the business you came on," she said cheerily as she closed the huge leather album and bustled out of the room with it. Sitting by himself, Nathaniel observed that all the birds in the Houdinis' incredible birdcage were asleep. He walked close to it, wondering why he had told Mrs. Houdini—she was a complete stranger really—so much about his aunt and mother and even his father.

Ribbit.

"What was that?" he asked out loud.

Ribbit.

Tiptoeing closer, he looked down and found a middling-size frog puffing itself up on the cage floor.

"Getting acquainted with Nicky?" The whisper startled Nathaniel. Mrs. Houdini was only inches behind him; she had walked back into the room soundlessly.

"Nicky is my husband's frog. He wandered in through the kitchen door and seemed very confused to Houdini,

27

very lost. Houdini calls him Nicky because the frog reminds him of Nicholas, Tsar of Russia. I met the Tsar, too, but I can't say he reminds me of the frog. Houdini is much better with faces than me."

Nathaniel began to laugh as Mrs. Houdini whispered, "Is there a reason why I am whispering? Can you explain it to me?"

"Not me, ma'am," he said, laughing more and realizing he liked Mrs. Houdini very much.

"So how much is the hat in question, young man?"

Nathaniel had not only forgotten the reason for his call, he had forgotten what he did with the bill. He patted his coat pockets, his trouser pockets, everywhere.

"Be gentle, sir, and you will find it. Wait, is that the bill on the floor over there?"

"Yes, that's it, I think," he said with relief. "By the birdcage."

"Birdcage! *Aviary* is the proper name for it," she said. "And if I may be so bold, what is your proper name?"

"Nathaniel Greene Makeworthy Fuller, ma'am."

She repeated it: "Nathaniel Greene Makeworthy Fuller. Heavens. Where does that name come from?"

Nathaniel automatically spilled out the family history he had heard his aunt Alice repeat so often.

"The first person in my family named Fuller made his living beating and cleaning wool during the reign of King Henry the Eighth, in England. He was so good at it that he became a wool merchant in London. And then he bought a big house in Norfolk—also in England."

"I meant *Makeworthy*," said Mrs. Houdini. "Is that a made-up name?"

"Fullers have been named Makeworthy since the time of Charles the First. The first Makeworthy Fuller came to Massachusetts with his wife, Patience, in 1635, looking for a place to practice the true religion in the New Jerusalem." He stopped suddenly, realizing he was reciting his aunt's words from memory. "I think they were unhappy in England, ma'am," he said.

"A good reason to leave—being unhappy where you live. My parents came from Germany, where they were unhappy."

Retrieving the wayward piece of paper from the floor, Nathaniel gave the bill to Mrs. Houdini.

She looked at it and began writing a check. "And were you named after your father?"

That question took his breath away like a punch. Every mention of his father did.

"I do not mean to be nosy, Nathaniel. If I may call you Nathaniel."

"Yes, ma'am, if you wish."

"Then please call me Bess. I feel like we are friends."

"So do I, ma'am."

There was a silence that he could not break; he didn't know why.

"Nathaniel, you and I share something very sad," Mrs. Houdini said while reaching out and grasping for his hand. "I lost my father when I was a little girl. It is still painful."

"My great-grandfather was named Nathanael—spelled a-e-l—Greene for a Revolutionary War general in our family, and Makeworthy for the first Fuller to come to New England. My grandfather liked the name but not the spelling, so my father was Nathaniel—i-e-l—Greene Makeworthy Fuller the Third."

He stopped. That was as much as he wanted to say, or could say.

"And your mother?"

"She's Mrs. Fuller."

"Does she have many names, all with a story like yours?" Mrs. Houdini prodded.

"Oh, I see what you are asking. My mother's name is Deborah."

"Nathaniel, I did not mean to upset you before. The name Makeworthy is rather unusual, to me at least. In our business, an unusual name is common—it can be the key to success. After all, my husband was not born Houdini. He made himself Houdini."

Not knowing what she meant but remembering to be polite, Nathaniel nodded in agreement.

"It occurs to me, Nathaniel, that you might be one of the very few people in New York who does not appreciate who Houdini is or what he does, due to your aunt's dislike of current events." Writing as she spoke, Mrs. Houdini carefully folded a paper into an envelope and handed it to Nathaniel.

"Now that our business is finished, let me give you this. Tonight, please give it to your mother with my compliments. Inside is your ticket to Houdini."

4

It was closing time when Nathaniel got back to the store. "How good you were *finally* able to return!" boomed Mr. Winchell. "The bookkeeper has left for the day, so we will have to leave that check in Mr. Bennett's office. Follow me."

Walking a pace behind, Nathaniel followed the older clerk. Inside the office door, away from the eyes and ears of other employees, Mr. Winchell wheeled about and glared down into Nathaniel's face.

"If I'd have taken the whole afternoon to go uptown and collect a check, I'd be lucky to still have a job. They'd dock me for being out all day. But Miss O'Reilly won't dock your pay. She won't clip you because you don't need the money, do you? You . . ."

Nathaniel knew that Mr. Winchell was fighting to keep his hatred in, to prevent himself from using insults that could get him fired if Nathaniel told.

"I couldn't help it, she—"

Nathaniel stopped before he made matters worse by saying Mrs. Houdini kept him there eating cake, drinking milk, and looking at photo albums. Not to mention the envelope she'd given him for his mother.

"She talked an awful lot, and she couldn't find cash to pay the bill so she had to find the checks. She just took forever. And the subway was slow."

"Take an El train next time," Mr. Winchell ordered. "The air in those subway tunnels will kill you; it's like going down a coal chute."

"I will," Nathaniel said as he slid out the office door, into the hallway, then through the showroom and out the front door. After waiting for the other employees to leave, he pulled the concertina folding gates toward the center doors, the first step in the nightly closing ritual.

Mr. Winchell had calmed down enough for the pair to do all the sweeping, tidying, and locking up in good time, but without passing a word between them. As the final step of their routine required, Mr. Winchell stood on the sidewalk and observed Nathaniel fastening the padlock on the outside gates. But at the click of the shackle, Nathaniel's still-angry superior raged again.

"Well, you'll be goin' uptown now, to your town house. You'll take a cab, won't you? What's a day's wages, heh? That's while I go home to Rivington Street and see what kind of scraps my mother got from the butcher today. I can't wait for my nice cold bath . . ."

Nathaniel walked to the corner and turned east onto Thirteenth Street before finally getting out of earshot. He laughed about the supposed advantages of being rich as he began the walk home. The trip to the Houdini house and back had used up all his pocket money, and he wasn't about to ask Mr. Winchell for trolley fare.

Nathaniel's house was nearly due north of the store. He could reach it by walking up Broadway and then Madison Avenue just as quickly, but he preferred to walk up Fifth Avenue if he was going to walk all forty blocks. He doubled back to Fifth after walking a few hundred feet, certain that Mr. Winchell was long gone.

From Bennett & Son to nearly Fiftieth Street, the avenue was filled with interesting store windows. Many were clothing stores, of course, but there were also bookstores like Brentano's, Mark Cross the harness maker, several art galleries, and F.A.O. Schwarz, the toy maker.

The street was clogged with people at this rush hour time of day, but few were interested in window-shopping. Groups of young women in high-collared shirtwaist dresses moved with great purpose — singly and in tight clusters — toward the subway or El or streetcar that would carry them home to Brooklyn, the Bronx, or even Staten Island. Young men — in twos and threes — moved less purposefully. They seemed more interested in the young women passing by.

After Forty-second Street, foot traffic thinned. Fifth Avenue became the street of churches and mansions and rubberneckers. Rubberneckers were tourists who rode in the open-air buses that traveled up and down the avenues. As guides pointed out the "elegant residence of Mr. and Mrs. Vanderbilt" or the "palatial residence of Mr. and Mrs. Astor," the passengers moved as a group and craned their necks for the best view.

Interesting as the sights were, curiosity tugged at Nathaniel. Every four or five blocks, he peeked at the envelope Mrs. Houdini had given him. Each time, in very foreign-looking handwriting, it always proclaimed "Mrs. Deborah Fuller" as recipient.

She, and Aunt Alice, would both be eager to hear how he had swept the street outside the store a dozen times and dusted the display hats sitting on their pedestals and "observed closely" Mr. Winchell, which the younger Mr. Bennett told him to do whenever he was "lacking other useful occupation."

Reaching East Fifty-third Street, Nathaniel turned the corner for home. Fifty feet from the front door, he saw his mother pressed against the parlor window. He thought Aunt Alice was standing behind. Suddenly unable to control himself, Nathaniel ran to his stoop, bounded up the five steps, and pushed open the front door.

"Nathan, at last!" his mother said while wrapping him in a hug. "Did they keep you late?"

"I trust everything went well today, nephew." Aunt Alice always came to the point straight and hard.

"Well enough, I think," he answered warily. Nathaniel knew to be neither proud nor overly humble before his aunt. Any praise or fault-finding should come from adults.

"If my good friend Mr. Bennett is satisfied"—Aunt Alice paused for seconds—"then I am satisfied. Report your activities for us."

Nathaniel's mother and great-aunt loved to hear about events in the world of business—a world foreign to ladies. Aunt Alice would be satisfied that Nathaniel had settled the Houdini account. But Aunt Alice would not be satisfied to hear about Mr. Winchell's meanness and bullying. Or about Mrs. Houdini's unusual scrapbook. He might share those things later with his mother. He would give his mother Mrs. Houdini's letter then, too.

Eagerly devouring each course of a warm-weather meal—soup, fish, mutton, greens, and tapioca pudding— gave Nathaniel time to mentally edit the day's events and make them seem less exciting than they were.

That was a snap, really. He just never used the name Houdini, only "the customer" and "the customer's wife."

Both women were shocked by the customer's actions and quite sympathetic toward the customer's wife. How difficult it must be, they agreed, to be married to such a wild man.

So Nathaniel entertained his mother and aunt quite excellently until Jennie, the housekeeper, brashly interrupted dessert. She had discovered Mrs. Houdini's letter while brushing Nathaniel's business jacket, and knowing that letters are always important, Jennie rushed into the dining room and handed it to the addressee.

Nathaniel's mother fumbled with the envelope after Aunt Alice instructed her to read it aloud. After removing the letter, she began reading in a tremulous voice.

" 'Dear Mrs. Fuller. Please pardon my forwardness in advance. You are graced to have a respectful, intelligent, but in some ways undereducated son.' "

"Who wrote this?" Aunt Alice demanded. "Who is criticizing my nephew's education?"

In answer, Nathaniel's mother kept reading: " 'Forgive my humor. I say undereducated only because he does not know what my husband does, a sad condition for a boy his age. To remedy that, please come to the Keith's 125th Street Theater tomorrow evening before eight o'clock. There will be tickets at the box office for Nathaniel, you, your aunt Alice, and your escorts.' "

"How utterly brazen! A complete stranger expects us to attend a vaudeville theater?" Aunt Alice was agitated.

"Wait, Aunt Alice," Deborah Fuller said. "The letter is

not finished: 'This will be one of Houdini's only performances in New York this summer, and it will be special. Of course Houdini would tell you that each performance is more special than the last. He's a very modest man.' "

Mrs. Fuller grinned. "What a charming woman Mrs. Houdini must be." The look on Aunt Alice's face told Nathaniel she did not yet share that opinion.

Deborah Fuller looked for a long moment toward her son with an expression, he thought, that somehow combined surprise with . . . mischief? "Am I correct in thinking that the unnamed 'customer' and 'customer's wife' we've heard so much about were Mr. and Mrs. Harry Houdini?"

"Houdini is enough!" Nathaniel said vigorously. "That is, Mrs. Houdini said he likes to be called Houdini."

"Deborah, please do not wander. Read!" Aunt Alice's tone was sharp. She was agitated by this unwelcome intrusion of the outside world into *her* dining room.

Nathaniel's mother continued reading: " 'My husband and I have not been lucky enough to have children of our own, so we love to see bright young people enjoy themselves. We look forward to meeting you and your entire family tomorrow.' Signed Mrs. Harry Houdini. Aunt Alice, don't you think it's wonderful?"

"Deborah, do you know who this Houdini is?"

"Oh, yes. He escaped from handcuffs in the Woonsocket jail the year that Nathaniel was born. Then in

Hartford, he escaped from a straitjacket. Nat and I always wanted to see his show, but never found the time."

"He's a criminal, a jailbreaker, a lunatic, and he performs in the theater? People *pay* to see him do these things?"

"No, he went to the jail not as a prisoner but to get noticed—for publicity," Deborah said soothingly. "He was not well known then. He performed in a burlesque show—"

"Burlesque? You would take Nathaniel to an indecent show?"

Nathaniel knew that women did hootchy-kootchy dances and belly dances in burlesque shows.

"This is a vaudeville theater," Nathaniel's mother said. "The Keith is bound to have a family show. I would really like to go. Nathan, did he seem like a criminal to you?"

"No, Mother," Nathaniel observed, "and Mrs. Houdini is nice."

She really is nice, Nathaniel thought, so thrilled that he could have run all the way back to West 113th Street to thank her.

"Aunt Alice, I think we should go," his mother said firmly.

Aunt Alice sat utterly still and was unusually silent for far too long. Finally she said, "I cannot stop you from going, Deborah, nor can I prevent you from taking my nephew. I will consult Mr. Trane before making a decision for myself."

Nathaniel saw his mother stiffen at the mention of David Douglas Trane, Aunt Alice's spirit adviser. Her hand tightened around the letter, crumpling it. He thought she must dislike Mr. Trane. He hoped.

If Trane was coming tonight, the ritual started months ago would play itself out. Nathaniel would be sent to his room. Trane would fawn over Aunt Alice as Nathaniel reluctantly climbed the stairs. Trane would direct a private sneer toward Nathaniel, as if they were enemies.

The doorbell would ring again and again as guests arrived. They would all chat pleasantly, and then there would be silence. If people were speaking, they would be whispering. The silence would be Nathaniel's cue to sneak out of his room and listen from the landing.

He would see that the electric lights had been extinguished and replaced by a few candles. Soon the booming Indian-man's voice would fill the air. Then, the guests would call out names and ask questions. The Indian—Nathaniel knew the Indian was really Trane speaking like an Indian—would respond. Back and forth they would go for an hour or more. Everyone in the darkened room would have questions for the Indian except Nathaniel's mother.

But she wouldn't talk to her son about Mr. Trane. Nathaniel was afraid to ask Aunt Alice about him. He had once asked Jennie, the housekeeper, what was going on. Jennie said that her priest was sure that they were "calling up the devils from Hell" and that she should run from a house with "such blasphemous goings-on."

Nathaniel looked *blasphemy* up in the dictionary and was even more confused. It said blasphemy was "profanely speaking about God," but he could never hear anybody cursing.

Aunt Alice relished these evenings, but Nathaniel thought that his mother had grown sadder since Mr. Trane became Aunt Alice's counselor. He could not understand why Trane made the one woman happy and the other so sad.

Luckily, Mr. Trane was out of town and couldn't be reached until the next day. Aunt Alice did not like telegrams or telephone calls. "Telegrams mean bad news and telephones invite strangers into your house," she often said.

Maybe Trane would stay out of town and they could enjoy the evening at the theater without him.

5

Nathaniel's mother sent a note for his employer the next day. It did nothing to improve the situation with Mr. Winchell:

If it is not terribly inconvenient, could you allow Nathaniel to leave half an hour early this evening? We have unexpectedly been invited to the theater by Mr. Harry Houdini and his wife. Nathaniel's one-time early leaving would make it possible for us to dine before the theater.

Many thanks,

Mrs. Deborah Fuller

As it turned out, both Mr. Bennetts were thrilled to have Nathaniel and his family working on their behalf. Soon Houdini would be performing in—and endorsing—Bennett & Son hats!

Mr. Winchell made it clear that *he* would have gotten the tickets in a *fair* world. And that was only the beginning of his grievances.

"You don't think my mother that slaves all day and my poor little brothers and sisters wouldn't like to see Houdini?" he hissed. "And you don't think that I deserve to take them . . . and you don't think that *I* should introduce them to Houdini myself? I made the sale, didn't I?"

"But Mrs. Houdini invited me . . . and my mother and aunt. You cannot pretend to be me. And I cannot go and ask for more tickets."

Nathaniel's logical recitation of the facts only made Mr. Winchell seethe more.

"You're the boss's pet now, rich boy, but now isn't forever." Winchell sprayed out his words while his facial muscles were locked in a grin. Trying to mask his emotions made Mr. Winchell look like the kind of grinning demon Nathaniel had seen on posters for a dime museum freak show.

"The tables turn in life, they always do. And when they do, you'll find me behind you, just enjoying all the misery you get."

At that, Mr. Winchell looked past Nathaniel, abruptly walked to the front, and cheerily welcomed a customer through the door as if nothing had happened.

Nathaniel sighed, dreading an entire summer filled with saying nothing as Mr. Winchell jawboned. He would pay dearly for leaving early tonight, but he didn't care. He ignored Mr. Winchell's fierce stare and rushed home. To his surprise, he met his mother in the doorway. He could tell by her expression that something was wrong.

"Mr. Trane does not see why anybody should waste time watching a 'cheap, foreign gypsy like Houdini,' " Deborah Fuller said. "Your aunt Alice has thought and prayed over the matter, and of course Aunt Alice agrees with Mr. Trane."

Then his mother hastily pushed Nathaniel back onto the stoop, walked through the door, and pulled it closed behind her.

"But *I* do not agree with Mr. Trane," she said, stomping her foot for effect. "In fact, I do not give a fig what either of them says. I am declaring our independence for the evening. We will have dinner in a restaurant and see the show. Agreed?"

Agreed!

Mother and son, arm in arm, bounded down the steps and practically skipped away toward Madison Avenue.

Suddenly Nathaniel's mother stopped short. "Let's take hansom cabs tonight," she declared, "take them everywhere. We will be gay and carefree this evening. Agreed, Nathan?"

Of course he agreed. To prove it, he ran to the corner and hailed a hansom cab pulled by a small but sturdy-looking chestnut horse. He scrambled into the tiny, enclosed passenger compartment of the two-wheeled vehicle. He called out to the driver, who sat outside, high above the passengers, asking him to turn around and pick up his mother.

She climbed in with Nathaniel's help, and they nestled together. Mrs. Fuller called out the name and address of a restaurant. The driver acknowledged by cracking his whip in the air. Minutes later, they arrived at a rathskeller, a restaurant down in the cellar of a building on Eighty-ninth Street.

"I ate in this rathskeller many years ago. I had never had German food before, and it was wonderful," Nathaniel's mother said.

"Did Aunt Alice come with you?"

"No, Aunt Alice would never, no . . . I came with . . . I came with your father, Nathan."

"My father? Did he like German food?"

"Oh, Nathan, your father liked . . . no, he loved everything. I mean that he loved living and trying new things and going to unexplored places. Let me order for you, the way that he ordered for me."

They ate bratwurst, two different kinds of cabbage,

crispy potato pancakes, and then a slice of cake with three different kinds of chocolate.

Another horse-drawn cab took them to the theater on 125th Street in no time at all; there were very few cabs or private carriages traveling north at that hour. As they raced up Park Avenue, Nathaniel's mother whispered that the driver was going dangerously fast, but she never told him to slow down. Neither did Nathaniel, who loved the adventure.

Keith's Theater had eight glass doors, all propped open to let in cooling breezes. They saw the ticket windows on the left-hand side of the lobby and eagerly went forward. As promised, there were five tickets in an envelope waiting for them. Nathaniel saw his mother deep in thought and was puzzled until she spoke to the cashier.

"Please explain to Mrs. Houdini that we are thrilled, overjoyed, to see the show. We are returning three tickets because my aunt was taken ill and could not possibly come. I have my son as my escort and could ask for none better."

"Don't you worry, lady," the cashier said. "I never seen Mrs. Houdini, or 'him' for that matter, come near my ticket window here. But you'd better get movin' 'cause the show's startin' again soon."

Mother and son turned to hurry, but crossing the fifty feet to the auditorium doors proved difficult. The lobby was filled with displays about Houdini, displays they both wanted to examine.

First, a heart-shaped board five feet wide had more than a dozen sets of handcuffs, leg-irons, and thumb-screws affixed. Each imprisoning device had a label proclaiming where it came from—England, Egypt, Holland, and elsewhere. A straitjacket was displayed next to the irons with a legend explaining that Houdini had escaped from it and a prison cell in Boston in less than fifteen minutes. To the right of the straitjacket was a wooden packing crate. A sign indicated THIS IS THE CASE IN WHICH THE EXPERT SHIPPERS AND PACKERS OF BIGELOW & WASHBURN WILL NAIL AND ROPE HOUDINI UP NEXT SATURDAY AT THIS THEATER.

Behind these displays, hanging from the ceiling, were three similar life-size posters of Houdini. In one, Houdini was rope-tied and handcuffed. In the second, he was wrapped in chains held tight by half a dozen hefty padlocks. The third poster showed Houdini being padlocked by policemen into an oversize milk can, the kind of can Nathaniel had seen loaded onto trains bound for the city. In each, Houdini stared out with a look of confidence.

"There he is chained in London and there in Berlin and there in Paris, but he always escapes, doesn't he?" Nathaniel mused.

"He does, he does indeed, Nathan. The man who gave us our tickets implied that he is here this evening. But how silly, you *met* him yesterday, so you know that Mr. Houdini is here. We are here because you know Mr. Houdini," she said proudly in the loudest voice Nathaniel had ever heard her use. Several of the theatergoers milling around the lobby overheard and seemed impressed.

As they walked behind an usher to their seats in the third row, Nathaniel explained that if they met Houdini after the show, his mother should be sure to call him plain "Houdini," no "Mr." was needed.

The two of them happily settled in during the first act, which wasn't an act at all—it was a Nickelodeon, a moving picture called *Sardine Fishing in the Bay of Biscay*. It was interesting to see French sailors handling their boat in a storm and pulling up nets with thousands and thousands of little sardines in them. There were lots of other events shown, but it finally ended with the boat coming to shore at sunset. All the fishermen waved to the shore, and then the movie showed lots of women—all their wives and mothers—standing on the dock and waving back.

Next came Alessandro, a man dressed as a clown who pushed on imaginary walls and climbed an imaginary rope. The program called him a mime. Then came Carlotta, a singer of "Sensible Songs." After that came a much better Nickelodeon—*Papa Buys Fireworks, and Gets Burned in the End*. Papa certainly did get burned when a mean neighbor dropped lighted fireworks down the back of his trousers. Nathaniel could imagine Mr. Winchell pulling that sort of prank on him, or worse.

He was amazed by how many entertainers performed in one theater. The program claimed that Keith's had "Something for Every Taste," but it seemed to Nathaniel as if he and his mother were the only people interested in every act. At least, they were the only ones who did not get up and leave occasionally. They attentively listened to the mournful music of Essie, the Gypsy Violinist, laughed politely at the jokes of the comedian Albert Calvert, marveled at the juggling talents displayed by the Mirador Brothers, and enjoyed the funny accents, if not the jokes, of the comedy act Bella and Her Fella.

After Bella left the stage, the curtain closed. Then a man in a shiny red uniform with a big, stiff mustache walked across the stage very slowly. Reaching the center, he unfolded an easel, put a card on the easel with only one word—HOUDINI—on it, and then disappeared behind the curtain.

It seemed natural to Nathaniel and his mother that those still in their seats would leave the auditorium during this pause. Instead, people began filtering back in to their seats. They talked expectantly, in curiously hushed voices. Some just stared at the motionless sign in front of the stage curtain.

Finally, the man in red walked across the stage again, picked up the easel and sign, and walked offstage. Then the curtain opened partially and quite a few people gasped. Someone exclaimed, "It's the Ghost Cabinet!" Others muttered their agreement. Nathaniel's mother gripped his hand tightly. Why? All that Nathaniel could see, all that anybody could see, were three life-size squares of black fabric on wheels. The fabric panels were arranged to form a triangle with its point facing the audience. Was Houdini inside this ghost cabinet?

Suddenly Houdini appeared under a spotlight at the left-hand corner of the stage. He dashed forward, to the front of the stage, where he stopped and teetered over the orchestra pit below.

Backing up a step, Houdini raked the auditorium with his eyes and boomed: "Layyy-deees and gennn-tle-mennn, Houdini, the *World's* Greatest Mystifier, the man who has entertained millions and performed for *all* the Crowned Princes of Europe, has come here tonight to defy an impossible *challenge* made by these good men of the New Rochelle Wicker and Rattan Company."

Houdini raised his right arm and waved it at the stage curtain. At this command, the curtain drew back to reveal three men in overalls and canvas aprons. Houdini walked toward them. "Sirs, have you brought me an impossible challenge this evening?"

The workmen looked nervously at one another until the man nearest Houdini spoke. "We have," he said, very gravely.

"And can you certify that you personally made your device, and that I have never seen or touched it before?"

"That we can," the same man answered.

"Then let us see your fiendish contrivance," Houdini said.

The man in the red suit and big mustache returned,

joined by a clean-shaven man wearing an identical red suit. Each grabbed a panel of the cloth triangle and pulled it aside to reveal what looked like a large brown clothes hamper sitting in front of the triangle's third side.

"Ladies and gentlemen," Houdini announced, "rattan, as we all know, is fiber, very tough fiber, made from the tropical palm plant. In some less civilized countries, rattan canes are used to whip wrongdoers until their blood flows." Now running his hand over the hamper's lid, he continued. "Unless I am mistaken, this is no ordinary rattan hamper, is it?"

The basket weaver, more confident now, took a step forward from his mates and said, "No siree, sir, it certainly 'tisn't. We wove the longest, toughest pieces our foreman could lay hands to. And they're wove tighter than any basket I ever seen. That's tighter than a whiskey barrel, I say."

A few catcalls from the audience prompted the craftsman to modify his claim: "Near as tight as a whiskey barrel."

"Indeed," said Houdini as he scrutinized the basket. "There is *no possible way* I could cut or saw through that without the damage being obvious." Before the weaver could answer, Houdini sailed on. "And there are no nails, no rivets, no fasteners, *of any sort* holding the hamper together?"

He walked toward us in the audience saying, "Ladies and gentlemen, there are *envious* people—imitators and competitors—who insult my art by saying that Houdini escapes from wooden crates by loosening screws or popping nails, that Houdini saws or even dynamites his way out of locked safes and metal containers, that Houdini has keys and lock picks and tools hidden that help him escape. Lies! Houdini is no cheap trickster.

"On the other hand, *foolish* people say that Houdini communicates with the spirit world, speaks with the dead . . ."

Nathaniel nearly screamed as his mother's grip tightened around his hand.

". . . or that Houdini dematerializes out of a box and rematerializes offstage. I can assure you all this is utter nonsense. Houdini is no phony spiritualist medium."

Nathaniel's mother was breathing harder; she fidgeted in her seat.

"Houdini is an entertainer!" He grinned, showing all his teeth. There was complete silence as he looked up and down and side to side at the audience. "In all modesty, the greatest entertainer who has ever lived since biblical times. Behold. I will show you!"

One of the red-uniformed assistants asked for volunteers to come onstage and "verify the proceedings." At least a dozen men eagerly left their seats and climbed the stairs to the stage. Nathaniel was asking his mother what *verify* meant when he heard his own name called.

"Is Mr. Fuller in the audience? Mr. Fuller of the Fifth Avenue firm of Bennett & Son, will you please come forward?" the assistant with the huge mustache said.

Nathaniel looked to his mother, who made all kinds of faces, one right after the other—she was shocked, then uncertain, then smiling like it was Christmas morning and she was watching him unwrap his present, then reassuring. "Go ahead, Nathan. There's nothing to be afraid of."

Nathaniel didn't move, and she nudged him again. "Go ahead."

As soon as he stood up, people pointed, and some groused, "Look, he's just a *boy*" and "What does Houdini need *him* for?" Others seemed amused.

Nathaniel looked for the shortest way to the stage. He forced himself down the aisle. People patted him on the shoulder, the head; one man slapped him on the bottom and made him jump, causing a few people to laugh.

Nothing that happened when he was around Houdini was normal. Nathaniel did not like his knees shaking or his stomach turning upside down or strangers laughing at him.

"Ladies and gentlemen, pul-leeze," Houdini commanded. "Mr. Fuller represents one of the finest haberdashery firms in this country. Its customers include the mayor, the governor, and Houdini himself. Please give the sharp eye and fine mind of Mr. Fuller your applause as he joins the committee."

The audience obeyed; Nathaniel was stunned. All the laughing died down, a few people clapped, and suddenly the whole audience was clapping and cheering for him. It *was* magic. Houdini could turn people on and off like electric light or tap water.

A cold shiver ran through Nathaniel's body, and somehow that made him less nervous. He walked up the stairs and across the stage by keeping his eyes on his feet. He tried to hide among the ten or twelve men who had joined the rattan weavers, but Houdini wouldn't let him.

"Young man, you are here, along with these quickwitted, sharp-eyed volunteers, to keep watch over my every move. You have so impressed Mrs. Houdini that she said to me: 'Houdini, if anybody can catch you out, it is my friend Mr. Fuller. Let him watch your tricks closely.' "

Seeing that Nathaniel was tongue-tied, Houdini kindly covered for him. "Very wise, sir. Keep your judgment to yourself until this challenge is met."

Houdini then interviewed each of the "members of the committee"—asking their names, their businesses, and verifying that they had never met him before. Nathaniel thought Houdini practically bounced standing still. He was a big tomcat that frisked about like a kitten.

Houdini was wearing opera clothes—a long, shiny black coat, a stiff white shirt, and a very pointy white bow tie—like in many photos in the scrapbook. His head was huge, or at least his head seemed huge on such a compact body. Nathaniel was the only person onstage shorter than Houdini. His hair was thick and wiry like a scrub brush parted down the middle. Nathaniel noted how his eyes drew one in. All one could look at was Houdini's blue-gray eyes. Nathaniel sensed that all the other men—the other members of the committee—were thrilled to be there on the stage near this most unusual man.

It seemed that Houdini had been onstage longer than any of the earlier acts and had already been more exciting than any of them without really doing anything yet. When was he going to do whatever it was that he did?

As suddenly as that thought came to Nathaniel, the action started. While Houdini made small talk with the committee members, the red-coated assistants went to work. They handcuffed him around the wrists and the ankles and with another set of handcuffs connected the two sets of cuffs to bend him over. Several committee members picked Houdini up and laid him inside the hamper. As Nathaniel looked down, he thought that Houdini winked at him.

Committee members locked the hamper lid with six padlocks. The assistant in red with the great mustache poured hot wax into each keyhole, and as the wax hardened, a committee member scratched his initials in the wax. That way, the assistant explained to the audience, people could tell if the lock had been opened with a key or a pick.

The assistants brought several chains and pieces of rope onstage, and while the hamper was held in the air by the committee members, the chains were locked and the ropes were tied around it. The committee members needed almost no instruction. Either they actually worked for Houdini, Nathaniel thought, or they had seen this all before. If they had seen Houdini before, why would they pay to see him again? Then a clock that must have been three feet wide was lowered on ropes from the ceiling to the right side of the stage. It was a stopwatch, its face running from zero to sixty minutes.

"Mr. Fuller," a muffled voice said. "Mr. Fuller, is everything to your satisfaction?"

It was Houdini. Nathaniel summoned his strength to say, "Yes, it is. I am satisfied—"

But before he could finish, Nathaniel heard a few laughs from beyond the stage and sputtered to a stop.

"Then," said Houdini, "let the challenge begin."

Immediately the orchestra played and the monster stopwatch's second hand moved to mark the time. The assistants pushed the velvet triangle panels back into place, hiding Houdini and his makeshift jail from everyone.

Nathaniel wondered what to do now. The other committee members were talking quietly, mingling with the weavers who had made the hamper. They were staying onstage, so Nathaniel decided he had to stay, too.

Nathaniel liked the band music. Every few minutes, they started a new song. Nathaniel didn't recognize any of them because Aunt Alice refused to have a Gramophone in the house. She said that listening to music playing from inside a box was unnatural and would shorten life, although she never explained how.

At least she had given in to his mother's request to let

the Edison Company run electrical wires at the house—Nathaniel and his mother were glad to be rid of the gaslight. Gas was better than candles, but it was a dreary, yellow-colored light. Jennie had less scrubbing and polishing to do because electric light did not leave soot everywhere. But Aunt Alice had never decided which was more life-shortening—gas or electricity.

That's how Aunt Alice judged everything. Baths and Ivory soap were good because they would not shorten life. An awful lot of things were bad—Coney Island, motorcars, telephones, canned food, ice-cream cones, pocketknives. Worst of all was Florida weather.

Aunt Alice's husband, Nathaniel's great-uncle Arthur Ludlow, had gone to Florida a long time ago and died there. Doctors blamed the weather. Aunt Alice *often* said the doctors knew that Uncle Arthur would have lived to be a hundred if only he hadn't gone to Florida to buy land. And whenever Aunt Alice finished talking about her husband and the evils of going south, she retold the story of Nathaniel's father.

She had done everything she could, Aunt Alice liked to say, to stop Nathaniel's father from going south. He had joined up to fight against Spain with Teddy Roosevelt and his Rough Riders in 1898. Aunt Alice pleaded with him not to go: "Think of your wife if you won't think of me."

"Deborah understands that I must go; she supports me," Nathaniel's father told his aunt.

"If you go, you will die and break my heart," Great-

Aunt Alice warned, "and you will end my life. If you go to Cuba, you will shorten my life down to nothing. Listen to me."

Nathaniel's father refused to listen. He went to Cuba as a member of the First New York Volunteer Cavalry. He went to help liberate Cuba from an oppressive European ruler, just as his ancestor Nathanael Greene fought to free the United States.

But three months later a telegram arrived saying that Corporal Nathaniel Greene Makeworthy Fuller III had contracted typhoid fever and been evacuated to a hospital in Tampa, Florida. He had died in that hospital before Deborah Fuller's train arrived.

Nathaniel was thinking that maybe he agreed with Aunt Alice about southern weather when a voice rang out: "Thirty minutes! Thirty minutes!" Glancing at the big clock, Nathaniel saw that it was true—Houdini had been behind the Ghost Cabinet curtains for half an hour!

After the interruption, committee members continued to talk among themselves. Nathaniel walked up to one of the black fabric panels and listened. He heard the grating of metal, then a man deep-breathing: Houdini was fighting his way out.

Nathaniel suddenly remembered that he was onstage. Hundreds of people watched the curtain while he was thinking about his mother and his aunt Alice and his father. He hardly ever thought about his father and the typhoid fever. He didn't know why. He looked out into the audience to see if his mother was enjoying the show, but her seat was empty. Where did she go?

Combing the theater with his eyes, Nathaniel saw Mrs. Houdini standing offstage. She waved, calling him over.

"Nathaniel, you would enjoy the show more if you weren't so tired," she whispered. "I think that you don't stay up so late every night."

That must be it, he thought, I'm tired.

"I just asked a stagehand to bring your mother backstage so we can all sit together." She gestured to three stools behind her, and Nathaniel gladly hopped onto one of them.

Mrs. Houdini sat next to him. "When my husband gets himself out of this difficulty, your mother must meet him. Of course"—she giggled—"if he doesn't escape, I might ask to return the very fine derby hat that you sold him yesterday."

Nathaniel tried to laugh quietly. He couldn't help liking Mrs. Houdini, even though practically everything she did made him uncomfortable.

Now she touched a finger to her lips and looked on to the Ghost Cabinet. Nathaniel did, too, and soon found himself drawn further and further into the drama. His eyes moved regularly, rhythmically, back and forth, from clock to curtain and back to the clock again.

"Forty-five minutes. Forty-five minutes," an assistant called out.

Tension mounted in the last fifteen minutes. When it

was nearly a full hour that Houdini had been in the basket, Nathaniel was surprised to find that his mother was sitting on the third stool, next to Mrs. Houdini. She was staring straight ahead, but the women were whispering to each other. Mrs. Houdini looked more at his mother than at the curtain, and Nathaniel wondered what they were saying. Luckily, he looked back at the stage just in time.

The Ghost Cabinet's black fabric sides dropped to the stage. Houdini stood on top of the rattan hamper and crowed: "Will wonders never cease!"

The building practically shook with applause and cheers and whistles, as if there wasn't enough anyone could do to show appreciation.

Houdini jumped down and staggered to the front of the stage. His shirt was wet and smudged with dirt; one pant leg was torn, and his coat was ripped in several places. He waved grandly, and the assistants picked up the hamper and carried it closer to the audience. At Mrs. Houdini's urging, Nathaniel jumped from his stool and joined the committee's inspection.

Astonishingly, the hamper looked untouched. The chains and ropes were undone, but the locks were still locked, the wax seals untouched. When the lid was lifted open, a committee member pulled out all the handcuffs.

The workmen and committee members encircled the hamper, closely inspecting every inch of its visible surface. There were no gaps, no cuts, no nicks to be found. The

New Rochelle Wicker and Rattan Company employees who had made the hamper swore that it had not been tampered with. There was simply no way that he could have escaped. Yet he had.

His voice now hoarse and low, Houdini told the audience: "Ladies and gentlemen, I hope and pray that Houdini has entertained you this evening and proved again that he is the world's greatest mystifier. Until I see you again, remember: *Nothing on earth can hold Houdini!*"

And Nathaniel believed him.

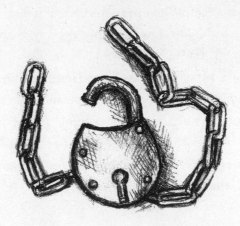

6

What happened next made Nathaniel's head spin. He was sure that his mother would say they had to hurry home. It was very late, and Nathaniel had to sweep the sidewalk in front of Bennett & Son, open six days weekly, at eight-thirty sharp the next morning.

But Mrs. Houdini swept his mother backstage. Both seemed upset. Gripping Deborah Fuller's forearm, Mrs. Houdini hurried past dozens of people and up two flights of stairs with Nathaniel following. Pushing open a door as she knocked on it, Mrs. Houdini entered Houdini's dressing room.

Nathaniel's mother held back at the threshold because Houdini was dressing—or undressing, Nathaniel couldn't tell which. All he wore were black socks with garters and his unmentionables—a white undershirt and knee-length drawers.

Both Houdinis were instantly embarrassed. Mrs. Houdini apologized, and the startled performer pulled on a soft, dark blue robe as Nathaniel's mother looked modestly away.

Nathaniel did not. He had seen pictures of strongmen outside dime museums before but had never seen anybody who looked as strong as Houdini. Houdini's arms and legs were enormous compared with the rest of his small body. His thighs bulged under his drawers. As he turned and slid his arms into the sleeves of his robe, muscles rippled up and down his back.

Nathaniel was shocked that all those muscles were blemished by cuts, dark blue bruises, and dried blood. Suddenly, he desperately wanted to know what had happened while Houdini was locked inside the hamper. How did Houdini manage to escape?

Before he could ask, Mrs. Houdini said, "*Ach*, forgive me, husband, I'm so upset. My dear new friend Mrs. Fuller, and her aunt, and young Nathaniel here—who I told you visited us from the hat store yesterday—may be in great danger. You must help them, Houdini!"

"Great danger?" questioned Houdini.

Nathaniel was surprised. What danger?

Houdini pulled two chairs together and guided Mrs. Fuller into one.

"Please, enlighten me," he invited.

Nathaniel's mother hesitated a long moment before Mrs. Houdini clasped her hand. "Don't hold back, child," she urged.

Deborah Fuller slowly shook her head, her eyes downcast. "I can't. I should never have burdened you, Mrs. Houdini. I cannot impose on you further. Nathan and I should thank you for a thrilling evening and—"

"Stuff and nonsense," said Houdini emphatically. "A burden shared is a load lightened."

"Are you uncomfortable speaking to my husband?" Mrs. Houdini asked. "Would it be easier if your son were not here?"

"No, no. It's because of Nathan that I broke down and said anything at all. Tonight has been magical. Nathan and I have had such a good time . . . it's been so long. And the way things are going . . ."

Mrs. Houdini pressed Deborah's hand between her own and said, "You've told me very little, but what you told me is *very* troubling. Take your time and tell us everything— everything you think is important. It will be a relief."

"And begin at the beginning," Houdini suggested.

After several moments' thought, she did.

Deborah said she was the only daughter in her family but had three older brothers. She took a commercial course in high school and became a clerk and typewriter operator for a law firm in Hartford, Connecticut.

"I fell in love with Nat—this is what I called Nathaniel's father—only days after meeting him. He had just graduated from Yale Law School."

She paused. Everyone was silent. A tear ran down each of Deborah Fuller's cheeks. Houdini took her free hand and enclosed it in a reassuring clasp.

"I am not an adventuress, believe me. I knew that I had no right, no hope, to think that a bright young lawyer from an ancient New England family could regard me as a prospective bride. I am a granddaughter of Bohemian *serfs*; my family *belonged to* a landowner until the Revolution of 1848. The Fullers were important in America two hundred years before my family had a right to leave the estate."

"My dear, it is not the blood in our veins but the spirit in our hearts that makes us noble," said Mrs. Houdini.

Nathaniel's mother nodded in agreement and forged ahead—telling how she and the young lawyer worked closely, how he realized that he was deeply in love with her and asked for her hand. They married and moved into a modest house in Hartford.

His legal career was progressing, but Teddy Roosevelt's call to "fight for high ideals" excited Nathaniel Greene Makeworthy Fuller III. He came home one day in late April 1898, jubilant that he had been chosen to be a Rough Rider.

"It happened so suddenly," Deborah said. "I had no idea that he had applied . . . It was a shock. I could not tell him I was going to have a child."

"He had no idea?" Mrs. Houdini asked softly.

"I was unsure myself. And I believed that it was bad luck to say anything too early," Deborah said. "By June, I was certain not only that I was pregnant but that I would be having a fine young son, my Nathan, so I wrote my husband and told him."

"The right thing to do," Houdini assured her. He released her hand, rose from his chair, and padded about the room.

"It was . . . but it unsettled my husband greatly. He talked about quitting in his next letter but knew he could not live with the shame of letting down his fellow soldiers. He also wrote to his aunt Alice. He told her that he had learned he was to become a father and asked her to help me."

"And she did," Mrs. Houdini suggested.

"She insisted that I close our little house in Hartford and move to her house in Manhattan. I did. It was the wisest course."

"Most sensible," Houdini agreed. He stopped pacing and sat down again.

"Almost everything went as planned," Deborah said. "The Rough Riders trained and steamed to Cuba. The Americans defeated the Spanish army. Cuba was freed. The troops came home triumphant . . . but my husband came home in a wooden casket before his son was born."

Clearly agitated, Houdini opened and closed his fist rapidly while trying to listen. He sagged back into the chair and unexpectedly pulled a deck of playing cards from his robe's pocket. Looking at Deborah Fuller, Houdini shuffled cards with one hand, again and again, very rapidly. Then he manipulated them, pushing single cards up and folding them back into the deck, cutting and re-cutting, rolling the cards quickly through his fingers—all without looking.

"If I am not doing something, I cannot concentrate," he said to excuse himself.

The room was less heavy now; Nathaniel's mother smiled and continued.

"Nathan became his great-aunt's only blood relative. She insisted that we stay permanently in her house. How could I refuse? My husband Nat liked to joke that he was from the poor side of his family, and I would say that I was just plain poor. My Nat left nothing but his personal possessions. I would have worked, but Nathan was so young. I could not care for him and work, too. Aunt Al-ice's offer of a home was a godsend.

"A year or so after Nathan was born, Aunt Alice in-sisted that I witness her new will. She will leave every-thing—her shares, her government bonds, her late husband's warehouses on Staten Island, her house on Fifty-third Street, her Connecticut cottage, and more— to Nathan."

"Two questions, if you please, Mrs. Fuller," Houdini said, and she nodded.

"There is no mention of you in this will?" he asked.

"No, there is not, but I would not expect to be designated. Certainly, my son will care for me if I need it," she said, smiling at Nathaniel.

"Exactly!" Houdini boomed. "I would not expect less from a one hundred percent son! To question number two: What is the dollar amount of your aunt's bequest, do you know?"

"At the time she signed the will, Aunt Alice suggested . . . that it was . . . nearly two million dollars."

Two million dollars! Nathaniel's worst subject was mathematics—one of the reasons Aunt Alice thought he should work in a store during his summer holiday. He did not know how much two million dollars was, but he had an idea how millionaires lived.

"Mr. Houdini, Aunt Alice communicates with the spirit world," Nathaniel's mother exclaimed nervously. "She talks with the dead."

"How very fortunate for her. It is a wonderful thing to make new friends at her age."

"Houdini, do not make jokes," Mrs. Houdini scolded harshly.

"I ask a thousand pardons," Houdini said. "This is not a new story for me, I fear." His eyes fixed on Nathaniel's mother. "Tell me about the trusted new friend your aunt made recently—the friend she values above all others. Is it a man or a woman?"

"It's . . . a man. David Douglas Trane," Deborah Fuller replied.

"Tell me his story now. I'm certain that it is an interesting one."

"Mr. Trane is the . . . unlawful . . ." She paused, looking at Nathaniel.

"Is he then the *illegitimate* son of a noble family?" Houdini asked.

"Yes." She blushed.

"Throw a stone in the air and it will land on some lost son of British nobility. Flapdoodle!" Houdini said, thumping a table. "Nathaniel, do you understand what *illegitimate* means?"

Houdini's question stunned Nathaniel. He had been quiet so long, absorbing the waves of information rolling over him. Puzzle pieces were being thrown at him too fast to fit into place. And the puzzle he was assembling was his own life story.

"Of course I do, it means Mr. Trane is a bastard," Nathaniel snapped. Things were swirling in his mind. He would never have used that word in front of his mother, or in front of any lady, just two days earlier. Everything was topsy-turvy, upside down.

"Language is *so* powerful," Houdini intervened. "Sometimes a word said aloud has less power than the same word unspoken. Do you agree, Mrs. Fuller? Now, the word I used is correct but still unpleasant. The word you used, Nathaniel, is correct for cutpurses and burglars and other low types, but offensive to your mother and my wife and myself."

Nathaniel started to apologize, but Houdini cut him off. "A lesson learned. Enough! Remember this: Inferiority is the mother of all profanity. And tiredness makes fools of us all.

"Bess, my dear heart, I need some of your incomparable cold chicken and berry pie. Our guests do, too. I will dress while you get a hackney—I am sure at least one nighthawk is waiting outside for a fare—and take them to two seventy-eight for a midnight supper. No objections."

"Mr. Houdini, did you hurt yourself—escaping from that case?" Nathaniel asked unexpectedly. "I saw cuts and bruises before."

"I guess you did see them. Well, those workmen from New Rochelle spent days making that fine rattan hamper. It is a beautiful piece of craftsmanship, and they were rightly proud of it. Would it be respectful for me to damage their artistry while performing mine? No! I had to be clever, as clever as only Houdini is, to leave it undamaged."

"How did you do that? How do you escape?"

"If I tell you that, my bread and butter would be gone. My chicken and berry pie, too."

Nathaniel drifted in and out of sleep during the short ride to 278 West 113th Street.

7

The next thing Nathaniel knew, it was morning. He was in a strange room but, undoubtedly, it was a Houdini room. There were posters advertising magicians and pictures of theatrical people all over the walls.

Through the wall, Nathaniel heard a typewriter clacking. Finding his clothes folded on a bureau, he dressed and walked next door.

He was astonished to see Houdini pounding away, his fingers hitting the keys like hammers driving nails. Houdini's desk faced away from the door, so Nathaniel stood in the doorway unseen, his eyes tracing an irregular circle around the bookcases. They went from the floor to the ceiling around three walls and were filled with books. On the floor were stacks of books, some piled three or four feet high, some so high it was a miracle that they didn't fall over.

"Nathaniel," Houdini said without looking up from the typewriter, "I am inspired every time I sit at this desk. It was owned by Edgar Allan Poe. He wrote some of his scariest stories at this desk. Someday . . . who knows?"

"Are you writing something scary now?" Nathaniel asked.

"Scary? Not at all. I am typing up my research for a book about sideshow performers. The chapter I'm working on is about swallowers—sword swallowers, stone swallowers. Did you know that there once was a performer whose signature trick was swallowing live frogs and regurgitating them still alive?"

"That sounds disgusting," Nathaniel said.

"Indeed it was," agreed Houdini. "I couldn't eat for a day after seeing his act. But right now you don't want to think about swallowing anything except my wife's sublime cooking. You should go downstairs and ask Mrs. Houdini for some 'ham or' and you will likely get 'ham and.' Also, tell my darling wife that I wait for her call."

After ripping a sheet of paper from the machine, Houdini smoothed it down on an inches-thick pile, fed another blank sheet in, and pounded away. Nathaniel backed out of the room and walked down two flights to the main floor. Remembering where the kitchen was, he walked in to find his mother and Mrs. Houdini having coffee. His mother beckoned him to a seat near her.

"Did you sleep well, son? You were so tired, the Houdinis insisted we stay. They sent the cab on home to let Aunt Alice know we were staying out for the night . . . Bess, this is the first night I have spent away from home in . . . since I moved to New York, I suppose. I hope Aunt Alice wasn't fretting over us, but if she was, maybe the cabdriver calmed her down. Nathaniel, are you hungry?"

"Very hungry. Mr. Houdini told me to ask for 'ham or.' Is that right?"

"You shall have anything and everything you like," Mrs. Houdini said, and walked out to the stairwell. "Young man," she cried up toward the third floor, "come for your breakfast or our guests will eat yours."

Returning to the kitchen, she said: "Years ago, when 'The Houdinis' performed in a traveling circus, we did everything but clean out the animal cages. Breakfast was ham or eggs, ham or pancakes, ham or toast—but never all of them, like you're going to have."

Houdini strode through the doorway and picked up where his wife left off. "We learned about the so-called friends of so-called spirits like Mr. Trane back then, working in the circus." Houdini grabbed Mrs. Houdini from behind and twirled her around in the air. "Light as a feather, bright as a button, sweet as a . . . a sugarplum! Dearest wife, life is too sweet to be soured by the likes of Mr. Trane. We must do something!"

Mrs. Houdini, on her own feet again, pulled her husband's head toward her, kissing his hair. Nathaniel felt bad. He never saw anybody treat his mother that way.

"Nate!" Houdini's voice boomed. "This is what I shall call you. I will not be confused, because my brother Nate has a mustache, unlike you. After you retired for the evening, Nate, your mother told us where you and she stand. And that is a perilous place. Through no fault of your aunt or your mother or you yourself, you are all standing on the edge of a cliff. You may be pushed over that cliff—"

"Mr. Houdini," his wife said in a cautioning tone. Nathaniel, or Nate as he was now being called, realized that she called him Mr. Houdini only when she was cross with him. She seemed to be cross with him a lot, even though they never yelled at each other.

"*Mrs. Houdini*, I will not mince words with Nate. You were right last evening—he and his mother are in great danger. His aunt? That is life or death. Nate, your mother told us her story last night, and I will tell you what it means."

Houdini explained that a friend had introduced Aunt Alice to a medium, Mr. Trane.

"Mediums are people who say they help the dead to communicate with the living," Houdini said, looking at Nathaniel. "Mediums claim to be messengers standing halfway between the afterlife and this world. But what they usually do is prey on the weak and vulnerable, offering a lonely widow like Aunt Alice hope while picking her pockets.

"I have seen hundreds of mediums perform their flap-doodle stunts: they ring bells, make tables wobble, make faces appear in the dark. Mr. Trane, devil that he is, says that your own father wants to speak with your great-aunt Alice."

"Can he really do that?" Nathaniel asked hopefully. "Can he let me speak to my father?"

"I firmly believe that there is a Supreme Being, Nate. I believe that there is a hereafter, an eternal reward that your father earned." Houdini's voice rose; he sounded almost as commanding as he did talking to the audience. "My mind has always been open and ready to believe at séances, but I have never witnessed real communication with the dead. Each and every case that I have investigated yielded two truths: True believers like your aunt are gullible—often heartbroken and desperate to believe. And people like Mr. Trane are cheats and frauds of the worst description."

"So I can't speak with my father."

"I cannot say . . . There is no absolute answer, Nate. The poet says that 'there are more things in heaven and earth' than we understand. Your dear mother told us a great deal about Mr. Trane and the way he toys with your aunt. That was enough to convince me that he is a faker of the worst description . . . a petty thief on his way to becoming a dangerous criminal. Mrs. Houdini, do you agree?"

"He is a very bad man, I fear," she said, looking from Nathaniel to his mother and back to Houdini. Nathaniel had never seen Mrs. Houdini so serious.

A sudden commotion of squawking caused everybody to turn to the aviary. Two of Mrs. Houdini's birds were fighting for the same spot on a perch. In a riot of noise, all the other birds picked sides in the argument, prompting Mrs. Houdini to rush across the room.

Nathaniel was relieved that the spell of seriousness was broken. He suddenly thought about how late he was and how difficult Mr. Winchell would be.

Mrs. Houdini billed and cooed until the birds settled down.

"Winsome Wilhelmina . . . Beautiful Beatrice . . . ," Houdini called brightly to get Mrs. Houdini's attention.

"Yes, Houdinski?"

Raising his hand to cover one side of his mouth, Houdini said: "The beautiful Beatrice Wilhelmina Rahner Houdini, 'America's Singing Thrush,' calls me Houdinski. She must be in love."

"Houdini, stay with the subject," Mrs. Houdini scolded.

"The subject *now* must be the whereabouts of Charlie Houdini. I fear that he needs exercise and fresh air as badly as I do."

"Charlie's in the garden, but first—"

"First, Charlie and I *need* exercise. Nate does, too. You, Mrs. Fuller, should send a telegram to your aunt explain-

76

ing your whereabouts. It is very inconvenient and too old-fashioned of your aunt not to allow a telephone in the house. But age must have its privileges. You should then call Nate's employer. Be discreet, Mrs. Fuller. Mrs. Houdini, you must telegram Atlantic City, telling my dearest mother and brother that we are detained—"

"But you should not change your plans on account of us," Nathaniel's mother interrupted. "We should leave."

Houdini raised both hands and put both index fingers to his lips.

"My mother will certainly miss us, Deborah, but she will enjoy the pleasant company of her other children. Favor us with your company."

Nathaniel's mother burst into tears.

"I will get my hat, and we will walk, those of us not needed here." Houdini opened the door and called Charlie. The terrier came enthusiastically.

"Please, Houdini, don't be gone all day. Nathaniel . . . Nate needs breakfast. And wear that nice new derby you bought from him," Mrs. Houdini added.

"What else would I wear?" he asked, jogging into the hallway and landing loudly upon each stair, Charlie at his heels.

"Deborah," Mrs. Houdini confided, "he would wear the same suit, hat, and shoes every day if I didn't hide his clothes and force him to change. Before an audience, he is immaculate. At home, he is a tramp. Or he would be if I allowed it."

77

Just as loudly, Houdini returned with a walking stick and wearing a stained, slouch-brimmed hat, the kind of hat cabdrivers and deliverymen wore to keep rain away. It was pulled down so far that it hid half his face. Signaling Nathaniel to follow, he was through the kitchen door and into the garden before Mrs. Houdini could ask where his new hat was. She shook her head and laughed.

"Houdini is a very easy man to make happy. For his birthday five years ago, I bought him a half dozen pairs of silk socks, very beautiful, very expensive. He thanked me a million times and put them at the very bottom of a drawer. And he never once wore them. When I say, 'Houdini, wear your silk stockings,' he answers, 'Yes, I must. They're so wonderful, such a thoughtful present.' "

"What a shame," Nathaniel's mother sympathized.

"Yes and no." Mrs. Houdini smiled. "Every year I spirit the socks out of his drawer, wrap them in paper and ribbons, and give them to him *again*. And every time he thinks they are new."

8

During the school year, Nathaniel had physical conditioning classes that he could live with or without. They got you outside when the weather was nice, but it was never as nice as the weather in Connecticut in July and August. And the exercises he did in class—such as point-to-point—were no fun. Running to touch a wall, then running to pick up a beanbag, then running to hand it off—what was the point of running point-to-point?

Walking with Houdini was harder and more interesting than that. Charlie, the little white-and-brown terrier, could hardly keep pace. Luckily, Houdini stopped every block or so to say hello to a street peddler or duck inside a store. He even carried a lady's grocery bags down the street and up four flights of stairs because "every mother is a saint."

With no obvious goal in mind, the trio walked eventually west to the Hudson River, then north and east to the campus of Columbia University. Houdini gestured to a bench, and finally they rested near the mammoth stone library building. The library had a long stone stairway leading to a row of Greek or Roman columns that seemed to hold up its giant dome. There were plenty of buildings in New York City as big and as beautiful, but Nate had never seen one with bright green lawns surrounding it on all sides. There were no students walking about on this brilliant summer's day. A few pigeons hopped at their feet, looking for food.

Aunt Alice said the only college a Fuller could ever attend was Yale. Nathaniel wondered if she knew about this beautiful school that was only a subway ride away.

"Man-to-man, Nate, it's time we spoke man-to-man." Houdini folded one leg over the other, draped his left arm on the back of the bench, and stared at Nathaniel. Charlie curled up against Houdini's hip, grateful to rest.

"When I was about your age, I went off to make my family's fortune. I rode trains like a hobo. I hid in empty freight cars, trying to reach Texas. I planned to make myself rich and return with hatfuls of money that I would empty out on the kitchen table for my mother and father."

"Were you poor?"

"We starved! I ached for food, but the less said about that the better. I learned a very valuable lesson then. I was not ready to take care of my family. If very nice people had not sheltered me, I would have frozen to death in the cold or died from hunger, have no doubt. I could never have become HOUDINI. I could never have given my mother a beautiful home."

Houdini paused. Nathaniel wasn't following. His thoughts had drifted back to the notion of speaking with his father.

"Man-to-man, Nate—your aunt is in danger. This villain Trane means to take her fortune, to throw you and your mother out of her house, to make you beggars. It has happened many times before, even in this city. I will not allow it to happen to you."

The force and speed of Houdini's statement hit like the quick punches a street bully throws when his victim isn't ready. Fighting to catch his breath, Nathaniel sputtered, "But . . . but . . . what do you mean?"

"This *creature* wants everything your aunt possesses. I have never laid eyes on David Douglas Trane, yet I know that he will not stick at killing your aunt—or you or your mother. He wants your aunt to change her will to make him, not you, her beneficiary. Thank your lucky stars that your aunt has resisted. But when she finally gives in, Trane will no longer need her, or your mother."

Nathaniel was choking on a rising tide of anger, rage, confusion.

"Breathe deeply, through your nose," Houdini counseled. "I just threw you into a bathtub filled with ice water. It will be easier now."

As if under Houdini's spell, Nathaniel's heart slowed, and it was easier to breathe. But everything Houdini said seemed wrong. Nathaniel disliked Trane, but had never guessed he was such a fiend. How could danger lurk so close to home while he saw nothing?

"Your mother told me that you are quiet but very smart. Can you be cool, deliberate? Your mother needs a red-blooded champion. Can you be that? This *is* a life-or-death affair."

"Of course I can," muttered Nathaniel thickly.

"Wonderful," Houdini said while uncrossing his legs and sitting upright. "Yesterday, your mother thought she was alone and helpless. Today she has three champions— my wife, myself, and, best of all, you. I can't sit so long when I am excited, let's walk again."

As they walked, Houdini explained the mysterious events in Nathaniel's house. Mr. Trane was holding séances. Aunt Alice and the unidentified guests were seekers of truth beyond the grave. Houdini also called them dupes, people who want so much to believe that they ignore reality, ignore their senses and the truth in front of them.

"Of course, this scoundrel Trane may be very good," Houdini suggested. "He may be an accomplished faker.

Remember that the two weakest senses are sight and hearing. It's easy to convince people that they see and hear things they really don't see or hear at all. I will show you."

Houdini searched his coat pockets and pulled out a piece of butcher's twine that he yanked taut between his hands.

"Now, Mr. Committee Member, hold the string while I show you there is nothing in either of my hands. I roll my sleeves up: nothing there. Now give me back the string."

He stretched it again, this time one hand in the air above the other. Making tiny circular movements, Houdini lowered the twine into his outstretched palm.

"You see that I only touch the string with two fingers here and it drops into my open palm, yes?"

When all the string was in the palm of one hand, Houdini waved his empty hand over the string and closed his palm.

"Behold a miracle! Pull the string from my hand."

Nathaniel grabbed the end and began pulling the string. It was knotted in a dozen places.

"How did you do that?" he asked. "Did you switch them?"

"My point is that it is easy to deceive your eyes by misdirecting them," Houdini said sternly. "You differ from your aunt and her gullible friends because you question. *You* want to know how Houdini does what Houdini does.

They believe that Trane really is doing whatever he says he is going to do. They do not question or even observe closely. They believe because they need to.

"Your aunt feels her losses deeply. She grieves the loss of her husband. She feels guilt that she lives while your brilliant young father does not. She has friends her age with similar concerns. Suddenly, a psychic appears, a medium who can reunite your aunt and her friends with their lost loved ones now and then for a few dollars. That is usually enough for everybody concerned.

"But not enough for Trane. He is turning your aunt's trust into a weapon to destroy your family. He will invent thoughts and desires, even accusations, for your uncle and your father. *They* will tell your aunt exactly what Trane wants her to believe—all lies.

"To make it all the more believable, Trane probably shakes the table, makes messages appear on a chalkboard, maybe he makes things fly. Hocus-pocus, nothing but cheap parlor tricks."

"You said that you couldn't say for sure if the dead could speak?" Nathaniel said. "I don't understand."

"Nate, if your father, rest his noble spirit, could speak from beyond the grave, what would he say? Would he come back to tell your aunt to harm you or your mother? Would he not want to speak to your mother before your aunt? Do you think he would want your aunt to make this wretched Trane person wealthy? These things are not possible, Nate!"

"No, not possible," Nathaniel agreed, his hope fading.

"But your aunt cannot see that. Filled with grief, she is easy pickings. No doubt, one or two of the sympathetic friends who attend Trane's séances work for him and help in the deception. Last week, your mother tells me, the situation reached a crisis: *his* lawyer wrote a new will for your aunt and asked your mother to witness it. Your mother begged your aunt not to sign the paper, to look for further 'proof.' Your aunt Alice agreed, but eventually Trane will overpower her. Unless we intervene, when your aunt dies, her home and wealth will go to Mr. Trane. Why? Because the so-called spirit of your father wants Trane to help other unfortunates reach their loved ones."

"But . . . if that's what he . . . my father wants?"

"On all I hold dear, I know that is *not* what your father would want, and I intend to prove it. Your aunt is a healthy woman, I am told. Trane will not wait forever for his reward. Besides, your aunt could recover her reason at any moment and throw Trane out on his ear. Therefore, I say that her life is in jeopardy. If I am wrong, I will apologize to all concerned. Gladly.

"But if I am correct," Houdini continued, "Trane has already concocted a new plan to sap your aunt's willpower and get her signature."

Despair tugged Nathaniel in one direction while the overwhelming energy and confidence of Houdini pushed him in another.

"What will you do?" he asked.

"*We* will expose Trane for the depraved criminal type that he is. *We* will help the police send him to jail, and restore peace in your house."

"How can I help?"

"You and your mother will help. You will pass intelligence to me, tell me what is happening in your home."

"Can't we ask the police to arrest Mr. Trane now?"

"He has done nothing illegal, nothing that we know of. And only we can prevent him from committing his crimes. Let's take Charlie home for his nap. We will make our own plans."

9

When Nathaniel, his mother, and the Houdinis gathered in the parlor, it was obvious that Houdini's plans were already formed. After explaining everyone's roles in what he called "the great upcoming melodrama," Houdini sent the Fullers home by cab. They braced for a scolding from Aunt Alice.

Instead, they found Mr. Trane settled in the parlor by himself. The massive wing chair by the fireplace had been shifted to face the front hall. "Why do you and the boy look so chopfallen, Deborah?" he asked. "Your aunt is not breathless to hear about your willful, thoughtless behavior."

Shifting his weight in the chair and clenching the armrests for support, Trane propelled his huge body up. It was such a violent movement that the heavy chair rocked backward. Most men, especially important men, were "prosperous" looking. Nathaniel knew that they were fat, but he had learned painfully that calling adults fat earned you an early bedtime.

Mr. Trane did not look comfortable with his prosperity. He acted as if he had just woken up wearing a strange body and he couldn't figure out how to move it about. He was always thrusting and thrashing, moving very suddenly and, just as suddenly, stopping, as he did then. He walked to the windows facing the street, drew back a curtain, and looked disinterestedly up, then down the street.

"Is Aunt Alice resting?" asked Nathaniel's mother.

"Send your boy to work, madam."

Nathaniel started toward Trane, shocked that he would order his mother about. She grabbed Nathaniel's arm and tugged him backward.

"I repeat, Deborah, send the boy to work. It is nearly noon."

Before Nathaniel could react, his mother said, "I was just thinking the very same thing. Nathan, I warned them you would be late, but you must get to the store before they think you've bolted. Go wash and change your shirt and hurry downtown, darling."

Turning her back on Trane, she rolled her eyes and winked at Nathaniel. He understood. She was reminding him to play along. ("Do not alarm Trane," Houdini had cautioned.)

"I will, Mother. I should go . . . now that *you* say it." He would play along in this spy game Houdini had devised, but Nathaniel wouldn't let Trane boss him about—not even as playacting.

He took the stairs noisily, opened and closed his door, then doubled back behind the stair railing to hear what Trane said next.

"Is Aunt Alice feeling poorly?" Nathaniel's mother asked.

"Why do you persist in calling dear Alice your aunt? She was your late husband's aunt. You are no blood of hers, just a guest."

"Sir, you have no cause to insult me! After my husband's death, Aunt Alice insisted that I stay here with her grandnephew. And—"

"And now, she knows better!" Trane thundered.

Nathaniel guessed his mother's tormenter was toying with a porcelain figurine from the fireplace mantel, not looking directly at her. Trane towered over his mother. He would tower over Houdini, too.

Mrs. Fuller broke the uncomfortable silence. "And what do you mean by 'she knows better'?"

"Perhaps it was for the best that you and the boy went off to a music hall last night. Best for Mrs. Ludlow, that is," Trane said.

"I should visit her."

"Mrs. Ludlow will not see you now," Trane cautioned. "Not ever again, were she less sentimental and tender-hearted. Her weakness is enormous. How fortunate for you and your boy."

"Would you be so kind as to tell me what happened here last evening? Did one of your 'sessions' alarm Aunt Alice? Is she well or ill? Please."

"Mrs. Ludlow is well, but exhausted. Her mind is now clear, her vision is now clear because the spirits have revealed the truth," Trane said dreamily.

"Then you had a séance last night."

"The most productive contact Mrs. Ludlow has ever experienced. All due to your absence, I believe. Without you here to inhibit them, the spirits communicated plainly. They let her see you in a new light . . . in the proper light, that is."

"And what light is that?"

"For the very first time, Mrs. Ludlow's dear husband, Arthur, was joyously able to break the veil. What a tale he told. It seems that your husband can find no peace on the other side. He is tormented by shame . . ."

What shame? Nathaniel craned from the upper landing to hear.

"*Haunted* was the word Mr. Ludlow used. Mr. Ludlow told us that your husband's feelings were too tender to tell Mrs. Ludlow, so finally Mr. Ludlow had to come forward and break her heart, yet again."

Aunt Alice's door opened down the hall from Nathaniel. He scooted toward the darkness and lay prone on his stomach, hoping he wouldn't be seen.

First, Jennie backed out of the room, noisily advising Mrs. Ludlow that she should stay in bed and rest. But Aunt Alice silently and slowly inched her way from the doorway toward the stairs and continued trancelike down to the parlor. Nathaniel had never seen his aunt come down the stairs in her nightdress and robe, never seen her thin, silvery hair uncombed. Nathaniel's mother and Trane waited silently as the elderly woman crossed the parlor, Jennie walking in lockstep right behind.

"Leave us, Jennie!" Aunt Alice ordered. As Jennie made for the kitchen, she stopped by the stairs and wagged a finger in Nathaniel's direction.

"Deborah, last evening was more disturbing than I can possibly tell you," Aunt Alice said.

"Mrs. Ludlow, you need not be so brave. Allow me to bear your burdens," Trane said.

"No, my dear David. You're too kind. It's my pain . . . my duty."

"Aunt Alice, I'm so confused, so worried about you," Nathaniel's mother said. "What has happened?"

"Deborah, your wicked deceit is at an end," the older woman replied bitterly. "Oh my heavens. I have longed so desperately for my husband, Arthur, to reach out and speak to me. And finally, when at long last he comes to me, it is to tell me that you are a liar. My husband said that you wantonly cheated my dear nephew. My nephew now spends his eternal life in tears—because of you!" she wailed.

To Nathaniel, Aunt Alice seemed hysterical, her mind as deranged as her hair. He barely heard his mother ask in a small voice, "But what am I supposed to have done?"

"My husband's spirit told me that Nathaniel is *not* my nephew's son, that Nathaniel is *not* my grandnephew—no relation to me whatsoever."

Deborah cried out in frustration.

"Her guilt, Mrs. Ludlow, is so great it overwhelms her," said Trane.

"I am not guilty . . . not guilty of that!" Nathaniel's mother yelped. "None of us is perfect . . . but I was never unfaithful to my husband. Your nephew was the world to me, he made me wonderfully happy. And he left me with a son, who makes me happy because he is so much like his father. Aunt Alice, how can you possibly believe that Nathan is anyone but your nephew's son?"

Both women were silent. So silent that Nathaniel wondered if his pounding heart could be heard by them.

"Do you think that the spirits lie, Deborah?" Trane hissed venomously. "Would you have Mrs. Ludlow believe that her husband came from beyond the grave to tell lies about you? You broke your husband's heart by pretending that the boy was his son. It is high time to clear the air and let the poor man's soul rest in peace. Admit your sins."

Deborah Fuller ignored Trane. "Aunt Alice, how can you possibly believe this? Nathaniel Fuller, your nephew, was the only love of my life. This is a horrible mistake."

"In the light of day, it is more difficult to believe you could wrong my nephew so terribly," Aunt Alice said. "Why would Arthur mislead me?"

"I don't know. But how are you and Mr. Trane so sure the spirit was Uncle Arthur? Aunt Alice, your husband has been gone so many years. How is it possible that he picked last night to tell you this incredible story?"

"Spirits of the departed don't perform on cue, like jugglers or acrobats," Trane said. "They don't come and go on schedules like trolley cars. But when they struggle to break the plane of eternity and communicate to mortals, understand this: their message is *always* true. I have been a conduit of spirits all my adult life, and I have never known one to dissemble, young woman."

"Maybe it wasn't really Uncle Arthur," Nathaniel said, coming through the doorway and surprising everyone. The women's antagonism melted before their concern for Nathaniel, but Trane was unmoved.

"Young man, these are not your affairs," he said. His voice was now caring and kind, as it usually was when Aunt Alice was within earshot. "It would be best if you went off to your duties at Bennett & Son."

Houdini was right: Trane was a very dangerous enemy.

"I won't go anywhere while you're saying things about my father and my mother."

"Clearly the boy understands nothing, and a good thing, too," Trane said.

"I damn well do—"

"Nathaniel!" his mother yelled.

"Well, I do understand. And he won't tell me what to do!" Nathaniel continued, ignoring his mother's warning.

"Stop!" said Aunt Alice. "Enough! This bickering is over. I must think more deeply. And you, Nathaniel, must go to work. I will not allow my nephew, or anybody living in my house, to inconvenience my friend Cyrus Bennett. You made a commitment to employment. Now, follow through. Deborah, help me upstairs. I feel unwell."

"But, Mrs. Ludlow," Trane said anxiously, "we have plans for this afternoon . . . Our trip, remember?"

Aunt Alice gave Trane a weary look. "Please postpone the plans, David. I am unsure, I need time."

"Unsure? You doubt the evidence of your own eyes and ears?"

Nathaniel wanted desperately to scream "Yes, you should doubt your eyes and ears!" remembering Houdini's lesson on the weakness of the senses.

"No, I do not doubt them," Aunt Alice admitted. "And I do not doubt your powers, David. I am not certain that I doubt anything. Or that I believe anything."

"It's not my wish to rush you, my dear. I merely thought you wanted to expedite the matter, to end your husband's discomfort and your nephew's painful suffering. That is all."

"Of course I do, of course I do," Aunt Alice repeated. Looking at Nathaniel's mother, probing her face, the elderly woman decided. "I want my nephew Nathaniel to tell me. He must. Yes, he must tell me the truth. I cannot act on my own."

"My dear Mrs. Ludlow, you know that may not happen. Your nephew is embarrassed and humiliated. That is why he spoke through your husband. Isn't that enough?" Trane prodded. "We cannot demand that the spirits jump through hoops for us, can we?"

"Dear David, I demand nothing of the spirits. I am grateful that they love me enough to come and speak to me. But I sorely wish that my nephew would speak for himself in this matter."

"I would like to hear my father talk about me, too," Nathaniel said.

"You may regret that, Nathaniel," she said sadly. "In any event, a day or two can be only another grain of sand in the desert. If Nathaniel has felt wronged for so many years, it is partially his own doing. If comeuppance is due, let him bring forward the bill. Yes, let him bring forward the bill. Deborah, please help me to my room."

As she did, Deborah Fuller walked past her son and said, "Nathaniel, hurry and go."

He was so quick to please, bounding up the stairs to get a clean shirt, that he didn't notice a faint smile crack one side of his fatigued aunt's lips.

10

Mr. Winchell was fuming, with good reason.

Nathaniel was Mr. Winchell's first assistant, the first person in his life that he could justifiably boss about. He *wanted* an all-around drudge—obedient, loyal, constantly toiling. Instead, Winchell found himself doing the drudge's work: sweeping the street before opening that morning, dusting hats, making boxes, and wrapping packages. Mr. Winchell's hostility toward his missing junior ripened by the minute as he contemplated making afternoon deliveries.

When Nathaniel finally arrived, Mr. Winchell knew that it was time to demonstrate who was the top dog. It was time to "put some stick about."

"What do you think you're at, huh? Slagging off on me? It's nearly one. *Your starting time is half past eight!* I ain't some greenhorn rube from Hickstown," he exploded, violently jabbing a finger in Nathaniel's chest. "Why, I oughta bash your—" The verbal outburst stopped as unexpectedly as it began. The street tough choked back his anger and became the proper junior clerk once more.

"I am not here to do your work, Mr. Fuller. Be warned" —he paused, and then with ice in his eyes and fire in his throat, Mr. Winchell finished his threat—"my little lord."

Nathaniel braced for more tongue-lashing as the Bennetts, father and son, glided through the doors in jubilant spirits. Beyond eating and drinking well, they had feasted on the afternoon newspapers' headlines: HOUDINI DEFIES IMPOSSIBLE CHALLENGE and HOUDINI ESCAPES FROM DEATH TRAP.

"Father," exclaimed the young Mr. Bennett, "there he is. What a triumph, young Fuller: to be singled out by Houdini, to be chosen a committee member, to—"

"To be recognized as an employee of Bennett & Son, Houdini's hatter," the old Mr. Bennett interrupted.

"The newspapers did not say that, Father. We should not jump to—"

"Conclusions? Of course we should. The man chose this lad because he worked for Bennett & Son; the very fact that Houdini knew the boy's employers makes it plain as the veins on the back of my hand that Houdini buys his hats here."

Nathaniel watched Mr. Winchell's mood darken even further. "Why didn't I deliver that bill myself?" he muttered.

"Houdini bought *a* hat here!" young Mr. Bennett agreed. "The trick will be—"

"To make him buy more—hats, matching gloves, and at least one walking stick," the father again finished the son's thoughts. "Once we outfit him entirely in Bennett & Son merchandise, what objection could he have to endorsing our products? We can write the testimonial ourselves and place it in every newspaper and magazine read by New York's gentry. It might even please us to relocate above that devilish Fourteenth Street borderline the newspapers constantly refer to," Mr. Bennett suggested, recognizing that Thirteenth Street was no longer the fashionable neighborhood it had been decades earlier. "The money is moving north. We must move with it."

"We could *give* him hats and gloves. That might—"

"Nothing is held so cheap as something got for nothing. Let us see if he's ready to buy before we start giving away the store."

Old Mr. Bennett became a whirlwind of action. He directed the senior clerk, Mr. Simpson, to assemble a package of hat designs, fabric samples for gloves, and drawings of very elegant walking sticks—all for Houdini's approval. Mr. Winchell and Mr. Fuller would deliver the package at Houdini's convenience. Both Mr. Bennetts retired to their office and then proudly reappeared to read a telegram that proclaimed the firm's commitment to render its prized new client a level of "personalized service unsurpassed by any other firm." Then it was back to business.

The afternoon dragged on endlessly for Nathaniel. His mother's confrontation with Aunt Alice and Trane gnawed at him. He longed to talk with her, but unless he went home that was impossible.

Houdini had insisted that if "anything unexpected, anything unusual touching this matter" happened, Nathaniel should telephone Houdini's home immediately. That was impossible, too: Nathaniel had been so upset he forgot to take Houdini's calling card out of his shirt pocket before changing, and now surely Jennie had thrown that shirt into the laundry. Houdini had scribbled his unlisted phone number on the card and told Nathaniel that it was his lifeline. Nathaniel imagined himself slipping out, dashing to the subway, and riding uptown to the Houdinis', updating them and returning to the store, his absence entirely unnoticed. Another impossibility.

Nathaniel and his family were in frightful trouble, and he could not do anything to help because he had slipped up. It made him feel useless.

So he passed the afternoon doing his tedious chores and staying far away from Mr. Winchell. At closing time, young Mr. Bennett warned Mr. Winchell and Nathaniel to be prompt the next morning and prepared to travel.

"Surely Mr. Houdini will see the mutual benefits of our

plan," said Mr. Bennett. "The public's awareness of Bennett & Son will be increased, and Mr. Houdini's wardrobe will be vastly improved."

Mr. Bennett folded his hands over his stomach and smiled heavenward. "Yes, mutual benefits will be obtained," he said as Mr. Winchell sullenly secured all the locks.

"That is all for this day. To your evening's enjoyments, young men."

Then they dispersed: Mr. Bennett got into the hansom cab that waited for him at the end of each day, Nathaniel walked north on Fifth Avenue, and Mr. Winchell headed south.

Plagued by fantasies of doom and death caused by his failures, Nathaniel did not hear a man's voice calling out to him from a doorway. The man, closely followed by a panting white-and-brown terrier, walked up alongside the dejected boy.

"A penny for your thoughts would be highway robbery," the stranger said.

"Houdini . . . it's you . . . oh, thank heavens," sputtered Nathaniel in grateful bursts.

"Forgive the unorthodox meeting technique. I understand from today's telegram that your employers wish to transform me into a walking advertisement for dry goods. Flapdoodle! Your employers would gain the prestige of Houdini's world renown—fame hard-won through years of study and struggle—and Houdini would gain . . . what? A pair of gloves? I repeat: Flapdoodle!"

Houdini realized that his humor was not infectious; Nathaniel seemed far from laughing. "What is wrong, Nate? Tell me."

"I lost your card," he replied.

"Easily remedied. I can afford to give you another."

"But I should have called you, called and told you what happened after we left you," Nathaniel said.

"Allow me to guess," Houdini suggested as he looked over Nathaniel's shoulder. "But no, allow me to lead while *you* tell the tale." With that, Houdini powerfully grasped Nathaniel's elbow and guided him to turn west onto a side street lined along each curb with wooden horse-drawn wagons and motor trucks. The drivers were industriously dropping off or picking up goods, making foot travel difficult. Houdini led a zigzag path as Nathaniel revealed Trane's accusations, his mother's desperate responses, and his aunt's confusion. As the details spilled out, Nathaniel realized that Houdini was turning him left at each corner they reached. By the time Nathaniel finished his narrative, they had circled the same block twice.

Houdini abruptly stopped and faced Nathaniel directly. Seizing his shoulders and staring intently, Houdini said: "Trust me, no damage has been done. We are better off now than we were this morning, but there is no time to explain. Learn from experience, steel your nerves. As my track coach used to say: 'Buckle up your courage and start the race.' And the race begins now."

"I will . . . I will," Nathaniel said sincerely. He was grateful both that he had not made matters worse and that he had not been scolded like a child.

"Excellent," Houdini said. "We must take care of unexpected business now. Charlie, do not stray," he cautioned the attentive terrier.

All three resumed walking toward Nathaniel's home. A few blocks later Houdini instructed Nathaniel to walk another block north, turn left, and wait. When Nathaniel turned to ask why, he saw that Houdini and the dog had vanished.

11

Nathaniel waited, as instructed, and pondered the unpredictable behavior of his . . . friend? Was Houdini a friend or a teacher or his family's protector? Nathaniel's concentration was broken by the grating voice of a newsie. "Extra, extra," the small boy shouted as he waved a newspaper above his head. "*Cat-a-strophic* crash at six-day bicycle race. Barone near death. Five other riders injured. Read all about it in the evening *Sentinel*."

The boy, weighted down by a canvas sack filled with papers, was approaching Nathaniel in hopes of a sale when Houdini reappeared.

"Nate, fortune has smiled upon us, unlike that poor Italian bicyclist Barone. Your colleague has offered to help," Houdini said brightly as he wrapped his arm around the shoulder of Mr. Winchell.

Yes, Mr. Winchell—the only person Nathaniel knew who hated him, other than Trane—was in league with Houdini. Nathaniel thought that he must have looked as stunned as he felt.

"Are we not fortunate, Nate, that just as we discuss the need for a trustworthy confederate your friend Leslie volunteers?"

"Leslie?" Nathaniel wondered aloud.

"That's right, *Leslie*," Mr. Winchell said, challenging anybody to make something of it. "They call me Ace, though, in *my* neighborhood."

"Ace," marveled Houdini. "Ace is powerful, direct, a fine name for a man of action. And I'm sure you are a man of action, Ace."

"I can do what's required," Winchell said confidently.

"How did you know we needed help, Ace?" Nathaniel asked.

"Well . . . it's like this . . . I—"

"Ace obviously saw us acting suspiciously near the store," Houdini suggested, "and decided to follow at a discreet distance. Observing that some weighty matter was being discussed by us, and knowing how brief our acquaintance was, he deduced that we might need help. Is that correct, Ace?"

Winchell visibly puffed up and nodded in agreement. Nathaniel realized that Houdini had noticed they were being followed—that was why they'd circled one block twice—and decided to flush the sneak out. But why on earth was Winchell following them? He had been far from the store when Houdini approached him.

In the two days—could it be only *two days?*—Nathaniel had known Houdini, he had learned a few things. Not disagreeing with Houdini was one of them.

"Since I have been out of the country, touring the capitals of Europe, for the better part of four years," Houdini resumed, "my reservoir of talented people in this city has dried up. Yes, like the old Croton Reservoir becoming the new public library, my old acquaintances are no longer there. We have need of someone who, at a moment's notice, must be trusted to follow a villain or deliver a vital message or even engage in more physical—even violent—action. Clearly, Ace is our 'hole card.' "

"That's right," Ace agreed with satisfaction. "That's me—your hole card."

Nathaniel thought the joke was about card games, but would not show his ignorance to Winchell by asking. He was uncomfortable with this new partnership, but how could he object?

Houdini's plan of action for Ace Winchell was simple: be ready and be alert. Winchell should be prepared to run errands, trail villains, do whatever Houdini demanded of him. He wrote down Winchell's address on Rivington Street. He gave Winchell a business card (without a phone number) and five dollar bills for expenses.

"Ace," Houdini said, "I am certain you can rest easy tonight. There will be no more action today."

"But, Mr. Houdini, could you tell me what exactly is going on, and who I might be trailing?" Winchell inquired.

"Tomorrow for that. I have an engagement this evening. And you will be late for dinner."

Before Ace could say a word, Houdini waved an arm wildly in the air and loudly called out "Hack, hack here" several times. A new taximeter auto, or taxi for short, was cruising down the avenue and swerved across traffic toward Houdini. Ace's eyes widened at the sight. Automobile taxis were noisy and smelly; passengers rode in windowless rear seats. But they were the latest thing—faster than horse-drawn cabs and a lot more swell than trolley cars.

"I don't like the idea of punking out on you just when things are heating up," Ace said. "But if you really don't need me, well, hot dog! Nobody in my family ever had a ride in one of these. I'll be *the* sight pulling up to my door."

Houdini pressed cash into the driver's hand and said, "Take this gentleman to Rivington Street—as speedily as safety allows."

Winchell eagerly disappeared into the passenger compartment, the driver shifted into gear with a screech of metal, and away they went. Houdini was silent. He watched the cab travel downtown for nearly three blocks before he spoke.

"Nate, you and Ace and I might become the three musketeers of Gotham. We have much in common—we are all three fatherless. His father left his family—ran away like a cur actually—and left young Leslie, Ace that is, as the oldest of four children with a mother too frail for garment work or maid work. Not only is your Mr. Winchell the provider for his family but he looks upon a career at Bennett & Son as his life's work. Quite different from you."

Nathaniel knew when adults were trying to make you feel guilty, and he feared a long lecture.

"Of course, he may be useful for some simple task. It's also possible that he is in the employ of Mr. Trane," Houdini said.

Houdini abruptly turned and stared at Nathaniel. "Never underestimate your opponent. Have you any idea why this Winchell followed us, Nate?"

"None," the boy replied.

"Well, we have no time for sideshows. The main event will be challenging enough. Agreed? Now that we know we will not be followed again, let us resume."

They walked at a leisurely pace, unlike other pedestrians rushing home to dinner. Houdini assured Nathaniel that, whatever Trane's plans were, they would not move forward that evening.

"Hurry home. Eat your dinner. Be a comfort to your mother and your aunt. And try to find that missing card of mine" were Houdini's parting instructions.

Except he also mentioned that there would be another séance tonight.

12

Nathaniel was flabbergasted that evening when he saw the first guest arrive. How did Houdini know that Trane would hold a séance tonight?

Poor Aunt Alice. She had the love and guidance of Uncle Arthur for thirty years. Then suddenly he was gone, gone without a chance to say goodbye. She transferred all her affection to a thoughtful, intelligent nephew who died the same way—suddenly, without a farewell.

Houdini said that Aunt Alice had nothing left to look forward to. She was reluctant to invest her love in a grandnephew like Nathaniel because she feared he would die suddenly, too.

Houdini told Nathaniel that Aunt Alice was certain

she had nothing to look forward to except her own death. She wanted comfort from her departed loved ones, assurance that they would welcome her "on the other side." That made her easy pickings for a conniver like Trane.

"Mr. Trane, may I introduce Count Helmut von Holstein to you," Nathaniel's mother said, reading from a calling card the unfamiliar guest had handed to her.

"My *dear* count, it is a *unique* pleasure to meet you," Trane oozed as he crossed the hallway and reached for the count's hand.

Lying flat on his stomach, Nathaniel was just barely able to spy all the action from the stairway landing. He saw the count stiffen slightly and step backward.

"It is vell to be here," said the count awkwardly in a thick accent.

Nathaniel thought he did not dress like the nobility in history books. The count wore an ordinary suit and tie like the Bennetts wore. He had long white hair and a huge white mustache. Most of his face was hidden behind the mustache and thick eyeglasses.

"Count, I do not know what your experience with groups of sensitives has been *on the Continent*, but I hope your evening with us will be profitable," Trane offered. "*This* group has had many, many profound contacts with the other side."

"That vould be good," said the count. Trane guided him to the parlor where Aunt Alice and the other guests waited, but stopped abruptly and turned to face Nathaniel's mother. "You are not needed, Deborah. Go to your room."

Before she could answer, he slipped inside and closed the door behind him.

Mrs. Fuller climbed the stairs briskly, turned toward her room, but stopped and motioned to her son hidden in the darkness. Nathaniel bellied his way across the landing and followed his mother into her room.

"Oh, Nathan," she whispered with great emotion. "What is this séance about? I had no idea it was happening . . . I have no idea who this count is. We *must* know what is happening."

"I think Houdini would agree," Nathaniel said. But he wondered how Houdini had been so certain that nothing would happen tonight.

"I am going to see what happens at these séances," Nathaniel said. And before his mother could disagree, he rushed to the servants' stairway at the end of the corridor. When Great-Uncle Arthur was alive, four servants had lived on the top floor and must have used these stairs all the time. Now there was only Jennie, and Nathaniel. He used them as a private shortcut from the kitchen to his room. That stairwell was the only place he could make any noise without disturbing his great-aunt.

He could not make a sound now, so he took the stairs on tiptoe. The stairwell was unlit and windowless; he used his foot to test each tread before stepping. As he carefully pushed open the door to the kitchen, he was relieved.

The room was bathed in moonlight. He navigated across without crashing into anything.

From the kitchen, he passed into the dining room. He could tell that the séance had not begun because light shined through the frosted glass of the pocket doors separating the dining room and the parlor. In fact, the doors were not completely closed; Nathaniel could see into the parlor. He slowly dropped to his knees to make certain he was not noticed. He crawled past the long dining table and positioned himself against a wall just in time. All the chatter in the parlor stopped abruptly, and the lights went out. The séance started.

"If we *all* are joined in a circle, we must *all* be very quiet," Trane told them. "Close your eyes and keep them closed. Concentrate, center your thoughts on your loved ones. Think only about that person you most wish to reach. Form an image in your mind. Hold that image. Reach out a hand through your mind. Yes, project a hand—mentally, keep the circle intact—project through the barrier of this flesh and bone, and *mentally* touch the spirit you long for."

As Trane continued, Nathaniel was pulled in. He was following Trane's directions. He imagined a picture of his father's face. Nathaniel tried to reach out into space, to reach beyond life itself.

"I am here, friend Trane. Eagle's Eye is here. I bring traveling spirits who need to speak, they are restless."

This new speaker broke the spell Trane's words had

cast over Nathaniel. The voice calling himself Eagle's Eye was obviously Trane talking like an Indian. Nathaniel remembered Houdini's words: "Why practically every medium in the world has a red Indian spirit guide is a profound mystery to me. I once met a Hungarian medium whose spirit guide was 'Mr. Chief Sitting Bull.' And they are so easily upset. An Indian brave who trekked through rain and snow wearing nothing more than a beaver pelt will blush if his motives are questioned. Nonbeings are very sensitive."

"Eagle's Eye, who have you guided to this house?" Trane asked, using his own voice again. "Who wishes to speak to one here?"

"Many spirits are with me, friend Trane, but they cannot speak."

"Why?"

"These spirits hide behind me like women frightened by battle. The circle is broken," Eagle's Eye said.

Aunt Alice and all the others insisted their hands were joined.

"The circle is broken by an unbeliever," Eagle's Eye thundered. "There is a deceiver in the room."

"It is not me," groaned Aunt Alice. "Arthur, if you are there, forgive me. I did not mean to defy your wishes. I believe you, Arthur, but I *must* hear it from my dear nephew before I can obey. Arthur, do you understand? Nathaniel, please come forward."

"Eagle's Eye, is it Mrs. Ludlow who offends the spirits?"

There was no answer, only silence. Before long, Aunt Alice blurted, "Oh, Arthur, do not abandon me. I need your help. I have always needed your help. Tell Nathaniel to come forward and I will do *whatever* he tells me to do."

"Mr. Ludlow say he is disappointed but not angry," Eagle's Eye said. "Your nephew is with him. Your nephew say he wants to speak, but there is a bad person in the room. They go now. They cannot stay."

"Please stay, please . . ."

Trane moaned and gasped for air; he pounded the table and made more noises. Finally, he regained his normal, greasy voice.

"This session is over. I cannot endure any more. The spirits are offended."

"It is my fault," Aunt Alice said grimly. "I refused my husband's request. I defied him."

"Rest assured, it is not you, my dear Mrs. Ludlow. Not you who insulted the spirits and caused them to flee," Trane said.

"No, Mrs. Ludlow, your dear Arthur understands. That is why your nephew came tonight: to help you understand, and obey."

"Heavens above," interrupted a disappointed elderly woman. "I've been here for every one of our sessions, and nothing like this has ever happened. What is the problem, Mr. Trane?"

"The spirits sensed a deceiver, a fraud, in our group. Since there is only one new member among us, it must be he."

"Vhat, me?" asked the count angrily.

"Surely it is obvious, sir," Trane responded. "I am uncertain what falsity the spirits saw in you, but I felt negative energy pulsing through our circle tonight. You are a disbeliever."

"I cannot accept these insults. I vas told that this vas a gracious, civilized home," the count said.

"My dear, what a thing to say about your host," said another séancegoer as she watched Aunt Alice slump in her chair.

"Ladies, allow me to escort our noble visitor to the door before more damage is done," Trane interrupted.

"I vill leave, most happily," the count said as he bowed to each person at the table and marched into the front hall. Trane followed, closing the door again.

Nathaniel could hear the count and Trane speaking, but the chatter of Aunt Alice and her friends drowned out their words. Nathaniel used Trane's absence to retrace his steps to the kitchen. As he opened the door to the back stairway, a hand gripped Nathaniel's shoulder. Dread blanketed him. Who could it be?

"Spying on the heathen doings, heh?"

"Jennie!" Nathaniel exclaimed as he turned and confirmed that it was the maid.

"What is it you're doing, young man? Shameful. Sneaking about and eavesdropping, risking your eternal soul with that man's mumbo jumbo. Bad enough those old ladies are involved—I pray for them—but you? I've a mind to tell your mother."

"Jennie, no," Nathaniel implored. Of course, it did not matter a whit whether she told his mother, but Nathaniel knew he should keep Jennie in the dark. "I just wanted to see what one of these séances was like. That is all, really. I saw more than enough tonight."

"Well," the housekeeper said, "no need worryin' your poor mother more than she is. And don't give me a look like that, young man. Do you think I'm blind, I don't see what's happening around me? Enough, go to bed."

Nathaniel needed no encouragement to leave. Seeing no light in his mother's room, Nathaniel sneaked into his. He fell asleep in a chair beneath a moonlit window, making notes and observations to share with Houdini.

13

After hearing Nathaniel's thorough report the next morning, Houdini slapped him on the back. "Excellent. One hundred percent observant. A good exercise for your mind, however unnecessary."

Unnecessary? That irritated Nathaniel.

"What do you mean 'unnecessary'?"

"Did I not guarantee that Trane's vile plans would not move forward last night?"

"You did."

"But you did not trust me completely, did you?"

They walked awhile in silence, Nathaniel watching the sidewalk as they moved leisurely toward Bennett & Son.

As Nathaniel left for work, Houdini had appeared beside him on the street, just as he had the night before.

"I guess not."

"But I was wrong, Nate. Not only did Trane forge ahead but he used me to do it."

"Used you?"

"He used my presence at the séance . . ."

"You were there?"

"And Trane knew it," Houdini said. "Trane knew that I would be there before I arrived."

"Before you arrived as *the count*?" Nathaniel guessed.

"Just so. Mrs. Houdini arranged the invitation, so it is unlikely he unmasked me that way. And my disguise was admirable, yes?"

"Well, I did not get a good look," Nathaniel replied. He remembered finding the outfit rather odd actually, but kept mum. "And it was dark in the parlor."

"The disguise was admirable," Houdini insisted. "I have used disguises many times that have never been detected. Trane was tipped off, as criminals say. He has an accomplice."

"Is it possible that the spirits told Trane who you were?" Nathaniel asked hesitantly.

"Possible? Where the possible ceases, the impossible commences. But nothing you observed last night was impossible. Trane spoke with a funny accent, so did Houdini. It proves nothing."

"The way he spoke . . . I don't know how to describe it."

"Oh, yes," Houdini agreed. "Trane was compelling, you were drawn in. Nate, the fact is that spiritualism is very good theater. It is cheaper than a ticket to Shakespeare—and easier to understand, too. But *it is theater*. Trane was performing."

"I suppose so."

"*Ach*, thank the heavens he did not levitate the table or make people fly around the room. Who knows what you would think?"

"Well, everybody believes—"

"Everybody attending Trane's séances believes just what they *want* to believe. He helps them with the crude hypnosis he works. In the dark, he lulls people into a trance," Houdini said. "Trane is a skillful trickster. And you are inexperienced. But no time for this now."

"I want to know how *you* know he is a trickster," Nathaniel insisted.

"You will, but first things first. We put the fire out first, then look to see what started it."

Houdini stepped up the pace—he wanted Nathaniel to be on time. Houdini talked rapidly, too. He told Nathaniel that Trane had no background, no history. The police, always willing to help Houdini, had no record of him. Telegraph inquiries to police up and down the East Coast and west to Chicago had produced nothing. Houdini had questioned employees at Trane's hotel, but that was another dead end. Inquiries at the bars and restaurants near his hotel were equally fruitless.

The morning was sunny and warm, but Nathaniel shivered to think how seriously worried Houdini was.

"You said that Trane used you. How?"

"To terrify your aunt. If she fails to carry out her dead husband's wishes—Trane's wishes—she will lose the chance to speak with him again. I have seen enough people bullied and confused to know that she is helpless.

"And this scoundrel Trane is supremely confident. He gloried in telling me that he knew I was Houdini and that Houdini was no match for his powers. He is likely a madman!"

"Why would he say that you were no match?" Nathaniel asked. "How did he know you were against him?"

"There he holds the upper hand. I am very well known in the world of spiritualistic mediums. Houdini has enlightened more than a few people who were bamboozled. Houdini has caught a few mediums in criminal deception; they are now in prison, fortunately."

Houdini walked through the front door of a greengrocer's store, leaving his words and Nathaniel hanging on the pavement. Moments later he returned and offered an apple from a paper sack.

"So you do this kind of thing a lot?" Nathaniel asked.

"I have helped people like your aunt before."

"And people like Trane—mediums—are they always fakes?"

"Nate, after years of research, nothing has convinced me that communication can be established between the spirits of the departed and us."

"You are sure no mediums are honest?"

"I cannot be sure about that. There may be honest ones who may communicate with the deceased. I have never met any, but I keep an open mind. That is scientific."

"I guess I just don't understand why you are doing so much to help us," Nathaniel said.

"Ah! There are two reasons, Nate. First, I am an entertainer, I perform illusions. But the public knows that I deceive them; it is part of being entertained. It is my duty—my *sacred* duty—to preserve the good name of illusion by unmasking dishonest tricksters. After all, it is only right that what brains and gifts I have should benefit humanity beyond merely entertaining people. And my second reason is just as good. Mrs. Houdini and I very much like you and your mother. We could not bear more hurt coming to you."

Nathaniel fumbled for words. Houdini, this famous man, cared for him, wanted to protect him and his mother. But before he could say anything, Houdini spoke again.

"I have a third motive, Nate. Last night that rogue unmasked me. Insulted me. He will pay. Nothing on earth can hold Houdini a prisoner and *no one on earth can make Houdini look a fool.*"

14

I am certain that Mr. Houdini will accept our offer when he returns to New York," the younger Mr. Bennett told the staff. "Mrs. Houdini—a lovely, refined woman—told me she was certain he would be flattered to be asked."

Nathaniel remembered Houdini talking about flattery in one of their lengthy conversations. "Flattery devours the soul, Nate," he said. "Someone must save me from it because I cannot resist it myself."

Mr. Bennett finished his speech and dismissed the staff. A normal business day began, but that lasted only a few moments.

"Don't fret about anything," whispered a voice in Nathaniel's ear. "I've got your back."

Looking around, Nathaniel realized that it was Mr. Winchell—his Ace in the hole.

"Now that *I* am on the case with Harry Houdini, we'll fix whatever it is that's wrong," Ace said confidently.

"I'm grateful . . . very grateful," Nathaniel said.

Ace steered Nathaniel to near the front windows. He shot glances around the room to make sure they could not be heard before he spoke.

"What exactly is it we are working on? He didn't have time to fill me in. He just said to be 'on call,' but for what?"

"It's a very complicated story," Nathaniel said.

"Exactly my point! I gotta know who the bad eggs are so I don't trip up and say the wrong thing to the wrong people. Here, look at this."

Ace Winchell pulled a thin brown leather-covered book from his coat pocket and slipped it to Nathaniel: *The Right Way to Do Wrong: An Exposé of Successful Criminals* by Harry Houdini. Flipping to the table of contents, Nathaniel saw that it was about burglars, pickpockets, and swindlers of all kinds.

"See, I went home and told folks that I was working with Houdini secret-like. Then a neighbor gave me this Houdini book about catching every kind of crook. And my neighbor told me it's all right stuff, too. He knows because he's a working man himself."

"A working man?" Nathaniel asked.

Ace's eyes narrowed as he stared thoughtfully.

"He does a little of this and a little of that, my neighbor. To support his family," Ace said.

"Your neighbor is a burglar?"

"That's no way your business, okay? It's hard to get a lunch-pail job if you're from the Five Points. It's enough to know that this book is the right stuff and that Houdini wrote it, okay?"

"Okay." Nathaniel realized that Ace, his comrade-in-arms, was very different from Mr. Winchell, his unbearable boss. Winchell was a street-smart operator trapped in a starched white collar and black tie. Which one would eventually get the upper hand: the clerk or the crook?

"Okay then," Winchell continued. "I don't see why Harry Houdini would waste his time on you if there wasn't some famous international thief in the middle, maybe somebody after your family's dough. So who's he on the trail of?"

"What are you doing here?" It was Mr. Simpson, the senior clerk. "You should never be standing on the floor together unless you are assisting a customer. And what is that book you are looking at?" he asked with a fully extended arm. Nathaniel handed it over.

As he flipped the pages, Mr. Simpson was shocked. "This is a book telling people how to commit crimes! Written by Mr. Houdini!"

Mr. Winchell tried to explain, but Mr. Simpson silenced him with a wave as he perused the book.

"Which of you brought this volume here?" demanded Mr. Simpson.

"I did, sir," Mr. Winchell admitted.

"I assume that you were going to share it with me, after showing it to your junior."

"Yes, sir."

"Excellent, Mr. Winchell. I was not aware that you read in your spare time. And in the future, make sure that you read only on your own time. I will now take this to Mr. Bennett. He may have to reconsider associating Bennett & Son with Mr. Houdini. I will tell him you brought this to my attention. Back to work," he said, and dashed to the owners' office.

"I'll be blowed." Winchell sighed with obvious relief. "I thought I was in for it."

Mr. Simpson's discovery had given Nathaniel a few precious seconds to think. He decided to tell Ace enough to make him happy, but leave out the story of his father and the talking spirits.

"Trane! The criminal's name is David Douglas Trane," Nathaniel said. "He is a dangerous international thief—"

"Danger doesn't worry me any." Ace swaggered.

"—and Houdini says that he is trying to steal everything my aunt owns."

"Everything! That's enough to buy this store . . . I'll bet that's enough to buy the whole A. T. Stewart department store down the block. You're filthy rich."

"I am *not* rich," Nathaniel protested. "And my mother

is not rich. My aunt is. But if Trane succeeds, all three of us will be poor, as poor as—"

"Poor as me?"

"That's not what I was going to say. I'm sorry that your father left your family and never came back. My father did pretty much the same thing."

"Your old man did a runner?" Ace asked.

"No, he went off to war. But he died there and he left us alone. Houdini says it is all the same in the end. Houdini's father died, too, when he was a kid."

As Winchell mulled this over, Nathaniel continued: "I would like to be your friend. After all, we have more in common than just our fathers. And we have to work together here. But even if we cannot be friends, I want to thank you for helping my aunt, and my mother, too."

Nathaniel thrust out his hand. Ace's face brightened slowly. Then he reached out and shook Nathaniel's hand enthusiastically.

"Okay, then," Ace said.

"Okay."

15

It was a busy day. Nathaniel made deliveries in three different directions and then went south to make a pickup. He realized that he was becoming a true New Yorker; he preferred to walk fast rather than ride. But now he took the Third Avenue Elevated train to his last stop. Elizabeth Street and back was too far a walk.

Elizabeth Street was part of a neighborhood called Mulberry Bend. Before Nathaniel's birth, the area's slum apartments were rented by Irish immigrants. The Irish moved out and were replaced by Italians so completely some now called it "Little Italy." Living conditions had not changed, though. Nathaniel had heard that a two-room apartment could house two families or a husband, wife, and five or six male lodgers. Tenants were lucky to share a hallway bathroom with forty others.

I'm glad I don't live here, Nathaniel thought as he picked his way through chaotic streets filled with people, animals, carts overloaded with vegetables and clothes and pieces of furniture. The smells of food cooking blanketed the air.

It seemed as if everyone lived in the streets. Hundreds of men and women were buying and selling on the sidewalks. They all spoke languages foreign to Nathaniel. Tiny children loudly played games like tag and hide-and-seek by racing under horses, around pushcarts, and into the spaces between buildings. Everything was motion and noise. Only a few broken-down old cart horses stood heavily still in the heat.

Number 26 Elizabeth Street was a tall, narrow wooden house with clapboard shingles that had been painted recently. As he climbed the creaking front stairs, Nathaniel thought that fixing them would have made more sense than painting the exterior.

Stepping inside, he immediately heard dozens of voices. Looking up the center stairwell, Nathaniel could see that every apartment door was opened. Even so, it was stiflingly hot inside. Every floorboard and stair riser seemed to groan from overuse. On the second floor, half of the ceiling and one wall were black with soot from fire damage.

Nathaniel knew that Ace Winchell and his family

probably lived like these people. He had never thought about it before, but he knew it. He realized there were things he knew perfectly well but never let himself think about.

It was just like the box of gloves handed him at the "factory" door on the third floor. From the doorway of a cramped apartment, Nathaniel saw more than a dozen women and girls hand-stitching pieces of leather. He would never see any of those girls in school, he thought.

Bennett & Son did not advertise that some of their finest goods were made by poverty-stricken children working in deplorable conditions. It was part of what customers knew but did not want to think about.

Back at the store, Nathaniel was given a rush delivery.

"Mr. Douglas, room six-twelve, City Hotel, is departing for Europe this evening. He needs several pairs of gloves but, curiously, no matching hats. So be it," said Mr. Simpson. "I would ask Mr. Winchell—he has more experience satisfying customers—but he is out and this must be done immediately. The customer was very impatient on the telephone."

"City Hotel is quite nearby," Nathaniel said. "I'll hurry."

"Good. Let the gentleman try on all of the gloves. Hopefully, at least two pair will fit his hand and taste. When he chooses, fill out a receipt for the total, be sure to record his complete mailing address, and collect the total."

"By check?"

"He said cash. Here is an envelope with dollars and coins if you need to make change."

Nathaniel deposited the money envelope in the breast pocket of his coat, picked up the box of gloves, and headed for the City Hotel. Minutes later he had traveled the five short blocks, bounded up the stairs, confirmed his appointment with the desk clerk, and ridden to the sixth floor in the elevator. He had taken very few elevator rides and still found them exciting.

When he knocked on the door of room 612, he was surprised to hear a gruff "Hold on!" Then the door opened. A man wearing overalls with suspenders and an undershirt beckoned "In here." He was not the usual gentlemanly Bennett & Son customer.

"Mr. Douglas?" Nathaniel asked.

"That's me, come in here and let me see the gloves," the man answered.

Nathaniel had taken no more than three steps into the room when he felt a very sharp pain in his head and knew nothing more.

16

Eyes closed, half conscious, Nathaniel heard a harsh voice. "I still say, if you want to hit the kid so hard, why don't you finish him here and now?"

"Enough discussion. I am not paying for your opinions," a second voice said.

Nathaniel felt a great pain in his head and even greater confusion. He tried to remember where he was. He couldn't move, and he felt something choking him. He wanted to open his eyes but feared that his head might explode.

"Look there," the man with the harsh voice said. "He's comin' 'round."

"This will be humorous," said the second man. "Nathaniel . . . open your eyes, dear Nathaniel."

Finally recognizing the voice, Nathaniel risked taking a peek. It was Trane, and the man in overalls. Nathaniel had a piece of cloth or towel gagging his mouth. He was tied to a chair with rope. If he was still at the City Hotel, he was not in the room he had seen from the doorway.

Nathaniel wanted to scream, but not for help. He wanted to scream at Trane.

"Bet that hurts like the devil, huh, kid?" the man in overalls asked. "Mr. Trane here ain't used to tappin' skulls. It's an art . . . sapping people but keepin' them alive."

Trane leaned near Nathaniel's face and spoke quietly, menacingly. "What makes you think I am concerned with keeping him alive, Cooley?"

"Well . . . of course you are," Cooley said nervously. "Temporary at least?"

"Planning is not *your* concern, Jack Cooley." Trane addressed Nathaniel again: "Would you like to join our conversation? Jack will take the gag out of your mouth if you promise to behave. No shouting. Be just as quiet as you were last night, or Jack will hit you."

As Cooley undid the cloth—it was a strip of towel—Nathaniel debated whether he should cry out and decided against it. He said the obvious instead.

"Jennie works for you."

"There, Jack, I told you this would be entertaining. So you and your shabby huckster magician learned nothing—*know nothing*—about me?"

"We know you belong in jail!" said Nathaniel defiantly.

131

"How harsh. You are not the only person, I sadly admit, to think that way. But none of you—especially you—will live long enough to see me behind bars."

"How did you get Jennie to help you?" Nathaniel asked. "She took Houdini's card from my shirt—that's how you knew it was him at your séance. And then she told you she saw me in the kitchen."

After a moment's hesitation, Trane said: "No danger in telling you now. You and your buffoon friend are so far behind me. Jennie does not work for me. She and Jack here work with me. Jennie is my sister."

"She's my wife," Cooley proudly said.

"But Jennie has worked in our house for years," Nathaniel said in disbelief.

"We have been separated for years, tragically. Jennie was here in New York—unbeknownst to me—while I trained to be a minister in the Church of Spiritualism," Trane oozed.

"Minister!" Nathaniel erupted. "You're no such thing!"

"Be quiet, boy! Lower your voice or you will regret it," Trane threatened, and Nathaniel was silent. "Many people are skeptical. They do not believe the spirits of their loved ones are real, so naturally the rejected spirits fail to communicate."

"Houdini says you're a crook. And so do I. I suppose that you kidnapped me and tied me up because I am skeptical," Nathaniel said.

"He's got you there," Cooley said.

"Dunce!" roared Trane. "Enough play. Put the bit back into this donkey's mouth."

Nathaniel opened his mouth to yell and realized his mistake immediately. Cooley jammed the towel in and tied it very tightly around Nathaniel's head. He gasped for air.

"Excellent, Jack. Make him uncomfortable," Trane said.

Nathaniel struggled against the ropes. He wanted to get free and rip Trane apart but knew it was hopeless. Houdini could free himself and overpower both of these thugs. But he was not Houdini.

"I have a busy evening planned, Nathaniel. Allow me to brief you, now that I have your attention," Trane said. "Your aunt Alice and your mother are enjoying afternoon tea and cakes at this very moment. Soon your mother will feel quite drowsy, in need of a nap. Jennie will help her upstairs and make sure it is a very long nap."

Nathaniel struggled violently against the ropes.

"Don't worry, kid," Cooley said. "Jennie knows her stuff. Your mother will wake up tomorrow feeling just fine."

"Jack, do not interrupt again," warned Trane.

"You're upsetting him too much. We want him quiet, don't we?"

Trane seethed. He seemed to choke on his own anger. A full, agonizing minute passed before he gained control of himself.

"With your mother out of the way, your aunt and Jennie and I will go to a special place—very special to your aunt—to hold a private séance. It will be brilliantly successful. Your father will attend. He will have such terrible things to say about your mother."

Nathaniel knew that Trane was baiting him like a cornered animal. He had to stay calm. He strained to hear every word Trane said and remember everything.

"After the session, Mrs. Ludlow will make a generous gift to advance the cause of spiritualism. That will keep us quite nicely for a few months, while I straighten a few things out. After I get your mother thrown out of the house and sent back to her to relatives in Connecticut, I can make all the necessary arrangements. Your aunt is not long for this life. She could pass in a few months, but it could be tonight, too."

"You don't mean that," Cooley implored. "That's way too dangerous . . . It's crazy to—"

"What is crazy is for my dear brother-in-law to question my judgment. Whatever I do is best."

"But why tonight?" Cooley asked.

"I did not say tonight absolutely. Possibly tonight, possibly months from now. It all depends," Trane ended with a sickening smile.

"What's it depend on?"

"The spirits, Jack. It depends on how the spirits move me."

"Oh . . . yeah. Very funny," Cooley replied.

"Something must be done about you, Nathaniel, and

your busybody friend. He will expect to pick you up at Bennett & Son later. Yes, Jack has done superior work observing your movements."

"That Houdini's a lot smarter than I thought he'd be," Jack Cooley said. "He mighta caught me tailing you if that guy from your store hadn'ta given me cover. When Houdini caught him, I knew to keep my distance."

"You will not return to work today," Trane continued. "Or ever. Houdini will search for you, I'm certain, to no avail. Here is the tearful letter you wrote to your mother explaining your disappearance. Jack, look at his surprise. Nathaniel did not know he was running away from home. Take off the gag, Jack. I *must* hear how he likes our plan so far."

Cooley hesitated for a moment and then unfastened the towel, saying, "Kid, if you make any noise, I swear I'll hit you harder than Trane hit you."

"What do you think of your letter? Was it difficult to write?"

"I never wrote that," Nathaniel protested. It was his own handwriting, but he had never seen the note before.

"A genius thinks everything out in detail," Trane said to congratulate himself. "I asked Jennie to borrow an old composition book of yours. For a few coins, an acquaintance of Jack's with excellent handwriting skills—a master check forger—copied in your hand the words that I composed for you.

"Let me ask, Nathaniel, did Houdini ever tell you he

ran away from home as a youth? He appears to have told quite a few newspaper reporters that he did."

"He did tell me," Nathaniel agreed.

"Brilliant! What could be better?" Trane was bubbling over. "In a week your mother will receive this letter from some distant point. She will show it to Houdini; he will be filled with guilt. Houdini will think *he* inspired you to run away. And your poor mother—knowing the accusations against her to be *utterly false*—will be heartbroken. Lovely, is it not?"

"But why . . . why?" Nathaniel asked in a choked whisper. "Why hurt my mother and me just to steal Aunt Alice's money?"

"Amusement," Trane said coldly.

"You accused my mother of being unfaithful to my father just to, what? To get the money faster?"

"Precisely. You are merely stepping-stones on the path to my happiness. I *am* enjoying your difficulties, but they are *your* fault. If you had not involved Houdini, none of this . . . folderol would have been necessary. But it is satisfying to see you squirm. None of you deserve to live in that house more than I do. I am earning the money."

"What are you going to do to me?" Nathaniel asked.

"You've read your letter. Maybe you will enlist in the army like your idiotic, idealistic father? But you're too young. Maybe you will join a circus or Wild West show. Who knows?"

"I am not going to do any of those things."

"No, of course not. But you may find yourself working as a servant on a coffee plantation in Brazil. How would you like to mine diamonds in South Africa?"

"Send me where you want. I will come back and find you."

"Point taken. It might be best for all of us if you and Jack take a walk by the river late this evening. You may fall in and never be seen again."

Nathaniel inhaled and tried to yell "help," but Cooley swung his rubber club too swiftly.

17

M r. "Ace" Winchell finished with a customer. Glancing through his sales book, he counted nine customers since Nathaniel had left for a delivery. It was taking Fuller a devilishly long time to show a few pairs of gloves. Ace wondered whether he was off with Houdini.

Opposing emotions tugged at the young clerk. *Mr. Winchell* would certainly have reminded his superiors that Mr. Fuller had been absent far too long. But *Ace*, coconspirator with Harry Houdini, continued to shield his comrade Nate. Ace doubted that someone like Nathaniel Fuller the Fourth could ever be his friend. The kind of people Ace knew visited people like the Fullers in the middle of the night, "invited" in through broken windows. But he thought that Fuller had the stuffings to be a right kind of guy; he didn't go whining to Mr. Bennett.

Ace saw Mr. Simpson coming across the floor with a look that spelled trouble. Not for him he hoped.

"I just had a disturbing telephone conversation," confided the senior clerk. "Mr. Douglas, City Hotel, room six-twelve, just upbraided me and our entire organization. He said: 'Since you have not sent your delivery boy yet, don't send him now. I will find what I need elsewhere.' I am flabbergasted, Mr. Winchell. What happened to young Fuller?"

Ace glanced toward the ceiling. Mr. Fuller had left for City Hotel—a five-block walk—nearly two hours earlier. Where was he?

"The boy's behavior has been erratic, but young Mr. Bennett likes him," Simpson said, thinking aloud. "And old Mr. Bennett is a family connection of his aunt."

Simpson looked again at Winchell. "There is no need to trouble our employers yet, Mr. Winchell. But it would be prudent to take some action. Mr. Houdini's crime book might offer a suggestion, but . . ."

"Why don't I just track him?" Ace volunteered. "I can walk the route, ask if anybody saw him. I can ask the hotel doorman."

"That's the spirit, Mr. Winchell."

"But I think we should try to satisfy the customer, too," Ace said. "I should take more gloves to the hotel."

"The customer was quite plain that he did not wish to deal with us," Simpson said.

"I just thought that, well, if Mr. Bennett hears we didn't even try . . ."

"You are right. Absolutely right," Simpson agreed. "Take a dozen pairs with you. Be tactful. Be discreet. And be back here before closing."

Minutes later, Ace stepped purposefully out the door and scanned the street ahead. It dawned on him that finding Fuller's trail would be impossible. No one loitered in this neighborhood. There were no street vendors with pushcarts who spent the whole day in one spot and noticed everything that went on. If Ace had been tracking Nate on Delancey Street or Canal Street or any street downtown, it would have been a different story.

He stopped at the corner tobacconist but got no help. A block closer to the hotel, he asked two hackney drivers waiting for fares.

"Do you think I'm crazy or plain lazy?" one driver asked indignantly. "I don't stand in one place for two hours. Go away, you fool."

The more he thought, the more sure Ace was that Nathaniel had met up with Houdini in the street and gotten up to something dangerous. And that they had left him behind. He kept a sharp eye for any sign of Fuller or the gloves. But he was more convinced by the minute that finding Nathaniel was a fool's errand.

"Have you been here all afternoon?" he asked the uniformed doorman of the City Hotel.

"I've been on duty since high noon, sir," the doorman answered. "Can I be of assistance?"

"Did you see a real scrawny kid—younger than me—in a suit go by about two hours ago? He would have had a bag like mine."

"I directed just such a person to the desk for information. Two hours ago precisely," the doorman said after consulting his pocket watch.

"Thanks," Ace said, completely surprised. The doorman pulled open a heavy glass door with ornate brass fittings. Ace passed into the lobby deep in thought, then turned abruptly and walked back.

"I would give you a tip for the info," he said, "but I don't have the price of a brick sandwich on me."

"I hear you," the doorman whispered.

Ace crossed the lobby to a check-in desk longer than the bar in most saloons. "I am here from Bennett & Son, to see Mr. Douglas in six-twelve."

"You appear to be disorganized at Bennett & Son," the clerk said. "You certainly are redundant." He motioned to another clerk and then repeated himself. As they sniggered, Ace's temperature shot up like a Roman candle. *Be tactful. Be tactful*, he told himself again and again.

"Be that as it may, I will go up to Mr. Douglas's room now," he said dryly.

"That is not possible," the desk clerk said. "Room six hundred and twelve has been occupied for several months by Mr. David *Douglas* Trane; we have no Mr. Douglas in residence."

Bells went off in Ace's head. Trane had called the store as Mr. Douglas twice: first to lure Nate here, then to run the staff off the tracks.

"And if Mr. David Douglas Trane is the person you were instructed to meet, you are far too late," the clerk droned on. "Mr. Trane checked out this afternoon."

"Did he say where he was going? Did he leave a forwarding address?"

"I'll see." The clerk wetted a forefinger and paged through the massive guest book. "No, he did not leave a forwarding address."

"Can you tell me where he lives?" Ace asked desperately. He had no idea what had happened to Fuller. Getting as much information as possible was the right thing to do.

"Young man, the personal information of our guests is obviously confidential."

"But I'm supposed to make a delivery," Ace pleaded.

"How many deliveries do you think the man needs from your store?" the clerk asked. "Mr. Trane received your other delivery boy hours ago. You should return to your store to straighten the matter out."

Winchell knew that Nate was in this hotel somewhere.

"Did Mr. Trane have any guests? Did he check in with anyone else?"

"Yes, actually. A rather unusual man checked in this afternoon and specifically asked for a room near the stairwell on Mr. Trane's floor. He left a deposit for the night, and Mr. Trane paid the balance when he checked out."

"I will go up to see him then. You see, Mr. Douglas—Mr. Trane, that is—already paid for this package. I should have been here hours ago, too. What room is he in?"

"Hmm, that would be Mr. Cooley in six-oh-two. I will call him and explain."

"Don't do that. It's better for me to explain," Ace said as he discreetly pushed a dollar bill across the countertop. "If he won't take this package—or at least tell me how to reach Mr. Trane—it's my job for sure. I have to go up myself."

The clerk casually placed a hand over the bill and said, "That's room six-oh-two, Mr. Cooley."

Ace thanked the clerk. He hoped the doorman had been outside when he bribed the desk clerk. And he hoped to see Nathaniel or Houdini before he had to account for that missing dollar to Mr. Simpson.

18

Ace Winchell thought about knocking on the door of room 602. But that wouldn't be likely to get him anywhere. Instead, he leaned his sample bag against the door to the stairs—for a quick getaway—tiptoed up to room 602, and put his ear to the door. A man was talking inside, but Ace could not hear clearly enough to understand what the man was saying. Ace decided the man was standing next to an open window and street noise was drowning him out.

Ace backed away and shot a quick glance up and down the hallway to see if anybody was coming. Putting his ear back to the door to eavesdrop, he realized the man's voice was getting louder. He must be walking toward the door.

"So, kid," Cooley said, "there's nothing I can do but take orders here. My wife won't cross Trane, she's his sister . . ."

Now I'm getting somewhere, Ace thought.

"I just have to do whatever he says," Cooley continued. "Probably Trane will call here before we leave and tell me to put you on the boat. You see, I have a friend who works on a ship leaving tonight for China. If we send you there, it won't be so bad."

The man must be talking to Nate. Trane and this man had trapped Fuller in room 612 and carried him here. Trane had left to rob the old aunt, and this guy was going to put Fuller on a boat to China. Incredible!

"He might call when he's done fleecing the old lady tonight. He might have a change of heart. Do you know if that old warehouse on Staten Island has a telephone?"

There was no reply.

"Just nod. You know the warehouse I'm talking about?"

Ace heard a mumbled "yes" and guessed that Nate was gagged.

"Good. Do you know if the place has any phones, so Trane could call if he changes his mind?

"No idea? Well, that's too bad for you 'cause the plan is that I take you out of here real late tonight—and don't think that's gonna be a picnic. But that's the plan: I knock you off, I carry you out of here in that trunk, and I lose you in the river. So you better hope Trane does call. That's what I hope happens."

Ace did not wait to hear any more; he dashed down the back stairs.

19

"Success! Mrs. Houdini, success at last!" Houdini
erupted triumphantly as he raced from the front door
to the kitchen. Accustomed to such outbursts, Mrs. Houdini poured the afternoon tea.

"It is a relief, my dear, is it not? This business will end
today. The clouds will lift from young Nate and his
mother and Aunt Alice. We can finally join my mother
and brother in Atlantic City. Should we ask those nice
people to join us, Bess? They need a change of scene."

"Houdini, you are miles ahead of me," Bess calmly said
as she stirred cream into her tea. "Is there good news in
that telegram you would like to share with me?"

"Someday, Bess, someday you will learn to read my mind. Yes, brilliant news. Frightening news."

"Houdini, please," Bess implored.

"You are right as always, Mrs. Houdini. Immediate action is required."

"Why?"

"My police inquiries about David Douglas Trane were fruitless," Houdini said.

"My memory is not fading, Mr. Houdini. I recall that, of course."

"But my recent inquiries concerning Jennie, the housekeeper, have produced pay dirt. Jennie is a dangerous, probably desperate, woman."

"The maid is involved," Bess said in disbelief. "She has worked in that house for years—how can she be involved?"

"Mrs. Houdini, we simply have no time to discuss it now. We must gather up the criminals before they do any more mischief. There is no time for tea."

Bess dramatically pushed her teacup away, folded her hands, and stared expectantly at Houdini.

"Good," Houdini said. "I will call my friend Captain Root and have him meet me at the City Hotel. I will ask him to send several officers immediately to detain Mr. Trane until we arrive with this evidence." He held up the telegram.

"Bess, you will go to the Ludlow home—"

"*I* will go, not the police?"

"Yes, my beautiful Bess. They need a friendly face and a calming voice, not a burly man in blue," Houdini said with a wink. "Besides, there is no danger there. Tell Deborah Fuller that the sun will shine again for her and her son and aunt. But tell the aunt nothing. Let me sort things out first. And be certain to say nothing Jennie can overhear."

"Houdini, how did Trane corrupt the maid? I must tell Deborah something."

"Jennie is Trane's sister! I am certain that will be enough to make Deborah cautious," Houdini said.

"It will, but what about Nate?" Mrs. Houdini asked. "Should a policeman bring him home?"

"No, no. He's fine at the store, out of harm's way. Just fill him in when he comes home. Now, I will call police headquarters while you put on a bonnet. Let's bring down the curtain on this melodrama and put a smile on everyone's face."

20

A Western Union delivery boy stood trembling outside room 602 in the City Hotel. Uniform cap in hand and telegram delivery-record book tucked under his opposite arm, the boy stared at the brass numbers nailed to the door.

"You know what to do," Ace Winchell whispered with irritation.

"If I get reported, they'll fire me," the delivery boy whispered back. "What if you're wrong?"

"I'm not wrong."

"If you're right, maybe he has a gun. What then?"

"Now you're afraid of a gun." Ace's irritation turned to

disgust. "Maybe I can get him to promise he won't hurt you or get your pretty uniform dirty."

"Can't you get somebody else?" pleaded the delivery boy.

"If I get somebody else, I'll tell *everyone* on the block you turned gutless on me. Every time a guy thinks he *smells* a nickel in your pocket you'll get beat from here to next week . . . if I tell 'em you're a chicken heart."

Deciding that the unknown was less frightening than the known, the delivery boy rapped brightly on the door. "Western Union. I have a telegram for the occupant," he said.

Cooley walked to the door. "Whosit from?"

Pretending to read, the delivery boy said, "Let me see, sir. The message is from a Mr. Trane . . . and is addressed to the occupant of this room."

Cooley spoke to somebody in the room—"That's what we've been waiting for"—and opened the door.

"Let me have it, kid," Cooley said.

"Please sign the book," the delivery boy said. Cooley grabbed the book and pencil and began to scratch his name.

Before he finished, they really let him have it. The Western Union boy gave Cooley a mighty kick on his right shin. As Trane's accomplice recoiled in pain—holding on to the record book—Ace charged him. He drove his head into Cooley's stomach. Cooley had a solid hundred pounds on Ace, but the blow upended him. The delivery boy joined in by grabbing a leg and pulling it up in the air. Operating with the practiced teamwork of street fighters, the boys rendered Cooley helpless with blinding speed. To finish him off, Ace hit Cooley with a hard rubber club similar to the one Trane had used on Nathaniel.

"Ace, I just gotta get back to work. Can I go now?" the delivery boy asked.

"Yeah, I'm fine here," Ace said as he undid Nathaniel's ropes. His friend grabbed his record book and scooted out the door.

"That must be real uncomfortable," Ace said, pointing to the towel in Nathaniel's mouth.

He deftly untied the knot holding it and pulled out the gag. As Nathaniel coughed and choked for air, Ace kneeled to undo the ropes holding his assistant's legs.

"I'm one up on Houdini now. You'da been gone down the river if I didn't come and rescue you," Ace gloated.

"How did you know?" Nathaniel asked. "How did you find me?"

"That's easy stuff for a man as smart as me. First—"

"Look out!" Nathaniel yelled as he rolled from the chair to the floor and rose unsteadily from all fours. Ace turned and saw Cooley—somewhat recovered—lurching toward him. Ace hesitated for a second and jumped aside, easily evading the groggy criminal.

"Run? Me run from a numskull clodhopper like him?" Ace joked defiantly as Cooley leaned against a window casement and gathered his senses. "This lug's too weak to get work as a bouncer at a tearoom."

"Boy, I don't know who you are," Cooley growled, "but when I'm done with you, a pack of street dogs wouldn't bother with what's left."

"Fuller, you better get on with your business," Ace calmly said.

"I will get you help, Ace," Nathaniel offered.

"No need. I can handle this blockhead until help arrives." Ace picked up a half-empty whiskey bottle Cooley had been drinking from and hurled it at him. Cooley ducked, but the throw clearly had not been aimed at him. The bottle flew over his head and crashed through the window.

"That will bring blue coats real quick. Go, Fuller! Take the stairs, run through the kitchen and out the back. Nobody minds; I've done it once already. And watch your back, Nate."

As Ace armed himself with a chair, Nathaniel took his advice and headed for freedom. When he reached the lobby, policemen were already running in.

"Room six-oh-two!" he hollered as he hoofed it through the front door. By the time he was a few blocks clear of the hotel, Nathaniel knew what he had to do next.

Before entering the first telephone booth he found, Nathaniel bent over, unlaced his shoe, took it off, and carried it in. After putting a coin in the telephone, Nathaniel dialed the number written on Houdini's business card. To be certain not to lose it, Nathaniel had hidden the card in his shoe.

Twenty rings later, a frustrated Nathaniel decided that nobody was home. He walked out, sat on the curb, and considered his options while lacing the shoe. He could go home and help his mother, but Cooley and Trane had both said she was not in danger. "Why lie about that after you say you are going to kill me?" asked Nathaniel aloud. "And Trane is crazy. I have to help Aunt Alice. By myself, I guess."

"Are you ill, young man?"

Nathaniel looked around and saw an elegant woman in a bright green summer dress with matching parasol and sun hat. She was staring at him.

"You are talking to yourself. Are you unable to stand?" the woman asked. "Joseph will help."

Standing behind her Nathaniel saw an elderly Negro servant whose arms were so filled with shopping boxes that Nathaniel could barely see the man's eyes peering over them.

"No, ma'am, I am quite fine—

"Joseph, do you need any help?" Nathaniel unexpectedly asked. "How can you see where you're going?"

The lady in green was shocked. "Joseph is my concern, not yours. I am convinced that something is ailing you, young man," she said sternly. "Is your home nearby? You should go home immediately."

154

"I should, ma'am, but I have something important to do."

"Suit yourself, young man. I was only trying to help."

That's my job now, he thought. Saying goodbye to the helpful lady and Joseph, Nathaniel dashed to the Union Square subway station. He boarded a downtown train and rode impatiently to the end of the line. Aboveground again, he ran to the Staten Island Ferry terminal and boarded a steamboat that would take him to Aunt Alice —and a showdown with Trane.

21

The flurry of activity that greeted Houdini outside the City Hotel signaled bad news. Clusters of curious pedestrians looked on as half a dozen uniformed policemen conferred with hotel employees. Two officers were locking the back door of a horse-drawn police wagon. Two porters swept glass from the street. Houdini caught sight of Captain Root and hailed him.

"Ah, there's Mr. Houdini, boys," the captain said to his fellow policemen. "Let him pass, make way."

"Is Trane in custody?" a harried Houdini asked.

"Bad luck there, Mr. Houdini; he's slipped us. Checked out long before," the captain volunteered.

"So what happened here?"

"Well, sir, it might be related, it might not," the captain said.

Houdini respected Captain Root. Root had an open mind; he liked to gather and analyze facts before coming to conclusions. That could be an irritant to a man as impatient as Houdini. Sometimes Root chewed on his facts too long for Houdini's taste.

"What do you know . . . so far?" Houdini asked.

"In the wagon here we have a rough type of fellow who the desk clerk *thinks* is involved with your Trane. But the rough fellow himself says that is not the case."

"Why is he in the wagon, then?"

"Well, the men I sent to latch on to your Trane are walking down the street here when a liquor bottle and most of a window land not twenty feet from them," the captain began.

"Extraordinary behavior," said Houdini. "This rough fellow threw the bottle?"

"Not at all. A young hooligan type threw the bottle."

"He was drinking?"

"Nope, so he says. The hooligan type says that he threw the bottle to raise an alarm—which he certainly did—because the rough type was trying to kill him."

"And what does the other party—the rough type—say?"

"He says that the boy broke in on him and tried to rob him," said Captain Root. "Both talking rubbish, I'll wager. I would end the whole affair right here with some curbside justice—just knock their heads together and send them packing—if it weren't for one curious thing. It's very curious that the young hooligan is the one dressed like the guest of a fine hotel while the other fellow—the rough one—isn't.

"I have determined one thing for certain, though—the rough type's room was paid for by your Trane. That's why I think they might be related."

"Might be? Of course this fellow is in league with Trane somehow," Houdini burst out. "Let me ride with him in the wagon."

"Well . . ." The captain hesitated. "Why don't we talk with him first?"

An officer used a rusty key to open the padlock and swung the back door open. Inside were two wooden benches attached to the wagon's walls. A large man in work clothes—the rough type—was sitting handcuffed near the door. A second figure—the hooligan type—was seated diagonally opposite him at the front end of the wagon. The youth's face was obscured in shadow.

"You there," the captain said, "we need to talk some more."

"More talk? Didn't I already tell you everything?"

"A good story is always worth repeating, isn't it?" Houdini asked. "And your story—"

"Mr. Houdini!" the youth interrupted. "You came."

"Ace, is that you?" Houdini stepped into the van to get a better look.

"It's me all right," Ace said with relief. "I told every thick copper here—"

"Watch your language, young man," cautioned the captain.

"Well, I must have told ten of your guys to call for Houdini. I guess one of 'em actually listened."

"How I arrived is unimportant. What happened?" Houdini demanded.

"I can tell you it's nothing to do with the pile of bushwa *he* told them," Ace said, trying to point at Cooley with shackled hands.

"You liar!" Cooley roared. "I tell you, he broke in on me and hit me while I was asleep."

As Ace and Cooley threw charges and insults back and forth, Houdini stepped from the van to talk with the captain.

"Captain, I vouch for the young man. He is working with me."

"I can't just let him go."

"Let him go? Not at all. Uncuff the lad and let him ride with us to your office," Houdini suggested. "Lives are at risk, Captain. I pray young Ace has information that will help us."

"And the other one?"

"If Ace cannot point us to Trane, that one will have to. Otherwise . . ."

22

Bess Houdini was frustrated. Her trip from Harlem to East Fifty-third Street had been accomplished in record time, she thought. But repeated knocks on the front door produced no response. With three people inside—Aunt Alice, Deborah, and Jennie—how could no one hear the racket she made? Not daring to fear the worst but still worried, she decided to update her husband.

There were no stores on Fifty-third Street near Madison Avenue. She walked west toward Fifth Avenue thinking that there must be a hotel nearby with public telephones in the lobby. A hackney driver pointed her north toward the Gotham Hotel at Fifty-fifth, where she closed herself in one of the ornate telephone closets so conveniently scattered about the city.

"Operator, please connect me with police headquarters," she said. Seconds later a desk sergeant answered.

"This is Mrs. Houdini, Mrs. Harry Houdini. Would you put me through to the captain, please?"

"I can't, ma'am," the policeman told her. "The captain is meeting with your husband."

"*Verflixt!*" she said.

"Excuse me?"

"When my husband arrives, would you give him a message? Tell Houdini that there is no answer at the Ludlow-Fuller home and I shall wait on the stairs until someone returns or until he arrives."

"Is there anything else?" the policeman asked.

"Yes, I wish that I had brought some sewing with me."

"Should I tell your husband that, too, Mrs. Houdini?"

"Yes . . . of course . . . he will want to know everything."

Mrs. Houdini walked back to the empty house and took up her position on the top stair. She would have brought Charlie for company if she had anticipated this turn of events. But he was better off napping in a neighbor's parlor. Mrs. Houdini decided not to think about the unknown perils that her husband and friends might face. She decided to enjoy the passing scene, but East Fifty-third Street in the late afternoon lacks interesting sights. It was too early for gentleman homeowners to return from work. The cooks and maids were all too busy inside preparing dinner to gossip in the street. Opposite her down the street, a bored coach driver leaned against his carriage. When a passing automobile backfired near the carriage, the horse whinnied and relieved itself in the street.

Mrs. Houdini remembered Houdini telling her that, before the invention of the automobile, horses in New York City deposited over two million pounds of manure on the streets every single day. She found herself wondering what kind of container it would take to hold all that manure, how many streets the containers would occupy, and . . . Shaking her head, Mrs. Houdini decided instead to concentrate on the dolls' clothing she would sew up for the Magicians' Club's annual donation to the New York Orphans' Home.

23

When the Staten Island Ferry docked at St. George Terminal, most passengers hurried to connecting trains that would take them home. Nathaniel approached a dockhand and asked for directions to the old Ludlow Shipping Company warehouse.

"There ain't nobody there, you know," the dockhand said. "It was a big business, they say. But that was before my time."

"I know," Nathaniel replied, "but how do I get there?"

"Up the hill, the road to your right. Just follow the shoreline and you'll bump into it. But it's empty," he warned. "Has been for years."

Nathaniel knew that it was not empty today. Trane had

brought his aunt Alice there because in the warehouse she would feel close to her husband. Arthur Ludlow had made his first fortune in that building. After the outbreak of the Civil War, the U.S. government desperately needed supplies—rifles, ammunition, compasses, telescopes, even shoes. Arthur Ludlow bought whatever he could and shipped it to his Staten Island depot. After delivering his supplies to the War Department, he collected a handsome profit.

Uncle Arthur had made many important business contacts during the war. When peace came, they helped him to build his second fortune. His friends advised him to invest in oil wells in the Midwest, a copper mine in Colorado, silver mining in Nevada, and even in the fledgling New York Telephone Company. To this day, Aunt Alice would not have a telephone in her house, but she had many telephone company shares in her safe.

The Ludlows were a sentimental couple. Even though the building was of no use to them, they kept it. And they had cleaners come every week to dust and polish the offices where Arthur Ludlow had made his first fortune. Occasionally they revisited the past by spending time there.

That ended, though, when Uncle Arthur died. Alice Ludlow never went to Staten Island again, but she would not break faith with her husband. The cleaners still came once a week. The past remained alive.

Nathaniel noted that the street was empty as the Ludlow building came into sight. The workday was over in this waterfront neighborhood; everyone had gone home. He cautiously tested the front door. It was locked. They must have used a side or back door. He turned the corner looking for it.

24

Bad luck here," Captain Root observed as he glanced at Bess Houdini's telephone message and passed it on.

"She must be very worried to make bad jokes at a time like this," Houdini said.

"Should I send a man from the neighborhood precinct to bring her here or take her home?"

"Send a man, yes. Tell him to call immediately if Nathaniel Fuller is with Bess. And make sure that Nate is with him when he phones—we must find out where Trane has taken them. If Mrs. Houdini is alone, please have the officer keep her company on the stoop—someone may return."

"Should I send a man to your home to pick up her sewing?"

Houdini was stunned. The captain had said something funny.

"Let's see what we can get from this henchman of Trane's who young Ace bagged for us," Houdini said without acknowledging the captain's unusual behavior. "And can we get Ace some dinner?"

25

Nathaniel found every door securely locked. Circling the building a second time, he decided the fire stair was his only hope. He climbed to the third floor and found a window unlocked. It was stiff from disuse, so he pushed it open inch by inch to keep it from creaking and alarming Trane. He crawled inside. The squeaking noises and sound of claws scuttling around on bare wood told him that the weekly cleaners did not remove the mouse—or rat—population.

Twilight illuminated the room well enough for Nathaniel to find his way into the much darker hallway. He could feel his heart beating but found it hard to breathe. He tiptoed down the long corridor very slowly, listening for voices at each closed door. There were none.

Nathaniel warily walked down to the second floor and saw yellow gaslight from a lantern flickering behind a door at the back of the building—Aunt Alice must be inside. But how could he enter the room unnoticed?

He approached slowly and saw a brass plaque on the door that said PRIVATE. That must have been his great-uncle Arthur's private office. He looked at a side door and saw another plaque—MR. LUDLOW. No light flickered under that door. He tried it and found the door unlocked. It must have been the secretary's office. It connected to the private office, as he had hoped.

He heard a voice coming from the private office. He saw light through the partially opened door, so he advanced. Just in time. The candles went out as Nathaniel neared the open door into the private office. Trane spoke.

"This will be a glorious session, my dear. Eagle's Eye assured me that the spirits will be comfortable here," the villain said.

"Oh, why did we not think of this weeks ago? Of course Arthur will be happy here, in his own office," Aunt Alice agreed. "I do wish Deborah had not fallen ill. She should be here, too."

"My dear, the spirits wish to speak—but *not* to her. With only you and me and your dear Jennie, your loved ones will certainly come."

"You know best. Can we begin?"

"We have a joined circle . . ."

Trane started the same long, hypnotic speech Nathaniel had heard at the last séance. He wondered if it ever varied. Still, it produced results quickly. In no time at all, Eagle's Eye, the Indian spirit guide, talked through Trane. After they discussed weather conditions in the spirit world, Uncle Arthur made an appearance. Actually, Eagle's Eye spoke for Uncle Arthur. Nathaniel used the time to sneak into the room and take up a position in the darkness behind Trane. Nathaniel could see that Jennie popped an eye open occasionally to check on Aunt Alice.

Uncle Arthur said he worried about Aunt Alice. "I was ignorant, Alice, but the truth has been revealed to you. Where I am now is blissful. You have the power to help hundreds, *thousands*, know the truth. You must do whatever Mr. Trane advises."

"I will, my dearest, of course I will . . . But I am somewhat confused."

"What confuses you, Alice?" asked the spirit of Uncle Arthur.

"The last time we spoke you were disturbed about our nephew," she said.

"Alice, the living cannot comprehend. One can be blissfully happy and disturbed at the same time—on this side of the Veil of Life. I must go for now; we will speak more. Just remember, do what Mr. Trane advises," said Uncle Arthur, speaking through Eagle's Eye, who was speaking through Trane.

"I will, Arthur. Of course I will," she effervesced.

"Wait. I see our nephew Nathaniel coming to me. Alice, he has stern things to say. Will you listen to him?"

"Of course, Arthur," Aunt Alice assured him.

Nathaniel swallowed hard. He was certain that this was all phony. It was cheap theater, like Houdini said. Still, he had a lump in his throat as the spirit of his father approached.

26

"If the boy and his aunt are in that building, Mr. Houdini, our Staten Island officers will find them," Captain Root said. "And they will scoop up your Trane, too."

Houdini did not respond. The captain was surprised that Houdini had barely spoken since their short voyage across New York Harbor began. He noticed that Houdini's expression seemed pained, and his color was decidedly pale.

"Mr. Houdini, are you seasick? You show the symptoms, but you sail back and forth to Europe all the time. It must be something else."

"Excellent, Captain. A one hundred percent skillful deduction," Houdini rasped with a wan smile. "If I had a cabin with a berth on this boat, I would be in it right now."

"This must be your first trip to Staten Island, then," the captain suggested.

"And my last, until they build a bridge."

"Mr. Houdini, come now. It must be miles from Manhattan and Brooklyn to the island. They can't build a bridge that long," the captain said.

"If we had an airplane, Captain, we could fly there. We could not do that five years ago. Mark my words—*someday* we will travel to Staten Island by horse or automobile."

They lapsed into silence again. The captain did not wish to argue with Houdini. Root thought a weakness like seasickness in Houdini was extraordinary. After all, Houdini overcame far more serious conditions. He could be locked and chained in fifty pounds of iron and jump into freezing water from a bridge and escape unharmed. He could be handcuffed and shackled to the bars of a locked jail cell. That cell could be protected by more locked steel doors in a prison that was "escape-proof." But sure enough, Houdini would walk through the front door minutes later.

Houdini had escaped from Root's own jail that way, after Root and the prison doctor had searched the escape artist for keys and tools. And Root himself had secured all the locks. Nobody ever escaped from the Tombs, but Houdini did.

The ferry neared land. Seagulls swooped above the

railing the two silent travelers leaned on. Houdini stared at the sun dipping toward the horizon and suddenly said: "Spiritualism is a fraud of the worst description, a menace to health and sanity, a *crime* that robs the deluded brains of suffering people."

"Bad luck that," the captain added. "It's not even the biggest crime we're expecting tonight."

27

What happened next at Trane's séance was worse than Nathaniel's worst imaginings . . . or better.

"The spirit Fuller is approaching," said Eagle's Eye. "He is very strong, very fearless. He says he must communicate now . . . it is so important to his beloved aunt. I go now. I leave him here."

Nathaniel's disgust for Trane's shenanigans was losing to his own anticipation. In utter silence they all waited for something to happen.

Nathaniel knew Trane did not have the power to bring back the dead. The man had tried to kill Nathaniel, he'd drugged Nathaniel's mother, and he was now lying to his aunt.

But the desire to hear his father's voice, to see his face—it was overpowering. He desperately wanted to talk with the father he had never even met. Could Trane, demon that he was, actually have some power nobody else, not even Houdini, possessed?

"Aunt Alice . . . Aunt Alice, can you hear me?" a man's voice said from far away. It was not Trane; it could not be Jennie.

"Dear heavens," Aunt Alice exclaimed. "I hear a voice, but I am not sure who is speaking."

"It is Nathaniel, sweet Alice," the distant voice said.

"Nathaniel was the *only* person who ever called me sweet Alice. It must be you, but your voice is so strange, so different."

"I am speaking through the veil that separates life and afterlife, sweet Alice," he said. "And the ether that surrounds the earth is a barrier to spirits also. Try to concentrate on my words. Think about me and I may penetrate the barriers. Think."

The next few moments were nearly unbearable. Then the voice said: "I have done it!"

Nathaniel's father was in the room—his face appeared behind Trane's shoulder. It was unbelievable, but it happened. Nathaniel's father's head and neck were floating in air behind Trane. He had no body—just his head and neck were there. His face looked like the pictures Nathaniel had seen so many times, but he looked ghastly, ghostly. A light glowed around him and made him look sickly, as pale as . . . as death, Nathaniel supposed.

"Saints be praised," cried Aunt Alice. "I feel faint . . . I can hardly breathe. It is you, nephew. Are you really here, in this room?"

"Maintain the circle," ordered Trane. "Keep your hands joined. I feel the spirit has joined us. Slowly, very slowly, open your eyes.

"Keep your hands in the circle! Break the circle and the spirit will disappear," Trane said passionately.

"Yes, yes. I will. I want you to stay, dearest Nathaniel," Aunt Alice said, blinking her eyes again and again until she was convinced that the ghostly head was really her nephew's. "Saints be praised, it *is* you. We have so much to talk about. There are so many questions I want to ask."

"Aunt Alice, I have very little time here. Listen carefully. My spirit is troubled by the wickedness around you."

"Wickedness?"

"Yes," Nathaniel's father said. "I *died* rather than admit it. But it must stop so that I can rest."

"You died rather than admit what? How can that be, nephew?"

"Aunt Alice, I never cared a whit about Cuba. I left because I could not bear my shame."

Nathaniel knew that was untrue. He had read his father's letters. They talked about the glory of helping people win their freedom. He compared Teddy Roosevelt to

Europeans like Lafayette and Kosciuszko who fought in the American Revolutionary War.

"*What* was your shame, nephew?"

"You know the truth, sweet Alice. Deborah shamed me. That boy who carries my name shames me," the spirit said.

"But how can that be?" Aunt Alice asked in disbelief.

"Do not ask me to explain! Believe me, you must!"

"I . . . I . . . it is very difficult . . ." Aunt Alice hesitated.

A fury had built inside Nathaniel. He wanted proof before he would listen to any more.

Nathaniel crossed the room before anyone realized an intruder was among them. He reached out and touched the disembodied head of his father. It was not flesh nor was it spirit. The head felt spongy, like very soft rubber. He touched the hair—it was rubbery, too, not hair at all.

"What the hell!" exclaimed his father. A hand pushed Nathaniel away.

A hand?

"Get away from me!" his father's voice commanded. The circle was broken as everyone seemed to be in motion. A pair of hands groped at Nathaniel from behind. A gaslight flashed on as Nathaniel grabbed the body attached to the rubbery head.

"My stars! Nathaniel! What are you doing here?" Aunt Alice exclaimed.

As he turned toward his great-aunt, the body attached to the rubbery head broke free. Turning back, Nathaniel could see the outline of a man dressed entirely in black—rubbery head in hand—sneaking out a back door.

"But you have driven away the spirit of your father . . . my nephew, I mean. What has happened?"

"This miserable meddling child has undone all my work," moaned Trane. "Boy, you will pay dearly for this."

"I believe we should all calm down," Jennie said as she put the lantern on the séance table. "Bickering won't get us anywhere."

"But Nathaniel has ruined months of work," whined Aunt Alice.

"I ruined Trane's work all right. And Jennie's, too," Nathaniel said. "Did you know that Jennie works for him?"

"She does not. What a ridiculous thing to say."

"Aunt Alice, that was not my father—you must see that now. That was some sort of rubber head that glowed in the dark. A man dressed in black was wearing the head and talking to you."

"But I saw my nephew. I spoke to him," his great-aunt insisted.

"But I touched . . . that thing. It was phony. As phony as Trane."

"Be quiet," Trane ordered. "Mrs. Ludlow is disturbed."

"I bet . . . I bet that you gave Trane a picture of my father so he could make that mask. And I bet that you gave him the key to this building. That's how his man with the head got in."

Nathaniel's great-aunt slumped. She looked at Trane for reassurance.

"My dear Mrs. Ludlow, you know that the spirits are often weak. They need help, some human intervention."

"Either my nephew was here or you are a *liar*, Mr. Trane," the elderly lady said with regret.

"My dear, spirits cannot always materialize at will. But the messages they send through me are true. I am a sensitive. They speak to me," Trane insisted.

"I fear this has been a charade . . . a play," Aunt Alice concluded.

"Cheap theater, Houdini calls it," Nathaniel added.

"David, this is getting us nowhere," Jennie interrupted. "We have to do something else."

Trane gave her a nod of agreement and fixed a glare on Nathaniel. "I am going to make you suffer before this night is over, boy. And I will thoroughly enjoy myself."

Trane and Jennie simultaneously started to close in on Nathaniel. He was ready for a fight, but a crashing sound from outside made them freeze. Voices called out "Nate!" and "Mrs. Ludlow!" Men were coming up the stairs. Trane and Jennie looked at each other with panicked eyes.

"Are those *more* spirits you invited to the party?" Nathaniel asked.

28

"Could anything be more impressive than the courage and resourcefulness—and cunning—these two young men showed today? Tell me!" Houdini challenged.

"Good luck there, very good luck," agreed Captain Root. "My apologies to you, Mr. Winchell, for treating you like a hooligan, but the circumstances did call for it."

Ace grinned. "If they could see me now, John Law asking my forgiveness. Ain't life amazing?"

"I pray that neither of you ever has to face danger again," Deborah Fuller said to Ace and Nathaniel, who were standing side by side behind the sofa she reclined on.

"A mother can only hope," Bess said, carrying a tray

filled with cups of tea and cocoa. Mrs. Houdini was acting as cook and hostess at the Ludlow-Fuller home. Jennie was in jail, Deborah was slowly recovering from the drugs Jennie had fed her, and Aunt Alice was dazed and listless but sitting upright in a high-backed wing chair. It had been a very long day, but there were still many questions to be answered.

"How did you uncover this plot, Houdini?" Bess asked. "Briefly please. We all need rest."

"You command, I obey," Houdini replied. "It was clear that Trane was a dangerous fraud when I attended the last séance he held in this room. I suspected that his claim to be the son of a noble family was bogus, of course, and the séance proved that he had no mediumistic powers either."

Aunt Alice shifted her head in Houdini's direction and seemed to listen.

"He knew I was disguised as the count and defied me to interfere with his plans. That told me, first, that he was not a man of goodwill and, second, that he had an accomplice in this house. All the searches I did regarding David Douglas Trane produced nothing—the man does not exist before he took up residence at the City Hotel. Possibly his accomplice had left a trail in life, I hoped. She had. Scotland Yard cabled me that Jennie McBride, a young woman identical in appearance to the Jennie employed here, was maid to an elderly widow in Bristol, England, eight years ago. One day a man described as identical in appearance to Mr. Trane came to visit Jennie. Neither the lady of the house nor Jennie nor the visitor was ever seen again. Expectably, the lady's safe was looted."

"What happened to the lady?" Nathaniel asked.

"Several years later the poor woman's remains were found—we do not all need to know the details."

"Why do you assume that this visitor was Mr. Trane?" Aunt Alice asked.

"It was an assumption, Mrs. Ludlow," Houdini said. "We lacked proof positive, until today. Mr. Cooley implicated his wife, Jennie McBride Cooley, and her brother—your Mr. Trane—in the crime. He told us that Jennie McBride came to New York with plenty of money. She met and married Mr. Cooley, and they lived comfortably until he gambled away her stolen share of the Bristol widow's fortune. To support them, she reverted to her maiden name and was perfectly happy working in your household and seeing her drunken husband as little as possible. Happy until her brother, David McBride, alias Trane, stumbled upon her working here."

Aunt Alice, her eyes intently focused on Houdini, took in the unpleasant revelations.

"We all know what a forceful personality this McBride, or Trane, has. He pressured Jennie into his plot to defraud you, Mrs. Ludlow. I am sorry to tell you these unpleasant facts."

"They will bother you no more, good lady," said the captain. "Trane and his helpers kidnapped your great-nephew. The city of New York takes that very seriously."

"But most likely the brother and sister will face capital charges in England. It was their misfortune to commit murder only months after the police adopted the Henry Classification System of fingerprints. The culprits who killed that Bristol widow left numerous fingerprints. Police from London are on their way to New York as we speak."

"*We* will keep Mr. Cooley," said the captain. "He will cool his heels in Sing Sing for kidnapping you, Mr. Fuller."

"Captain, what about that desk clerk at the City Hotel, the one who sent me to meet *Mr. Douglas?*" Nate asked. "Was he part of Trane's gang?"

"I don't suspect he was," the captain replied. "He just pocketed a fiver to help a guest play a joke on Bennett & Son. My men told the hotel manager to keep a sharp eye on the desk staff, just in case."

Aunt Alice painfully rose from her chair. Seeing that she was uncertain on her feet, the captain gave her his arm.

"The disclosures you have made take from me nearly all the hopes I have cherished," she said dully. "Perhaps it is best that the delusions I held should be swept away by one malevolent word, the word *fraud*. There is nothing left for me but to hope for the rest that death promises us."

Her words hung in the still, silent air.

Aunt Alice sighed very heavily. "I will go to my room now."

She and the police captain had reached the hallway when Aunt Alice turned back. "Nathaniel, you are a brave boy, a kind and generous boy. I should have seen how much like your father you are."

She turned away, and the captain helped her up the stairs.

Deborah was the first to speak. "I cannot ever repay the Houdinis. Nathaniel and I will always be indebted to you."

"Pish! Houdini loves getting himself into scrapes so he can escape," Bess protested.

"And let us remember that the genuine, one hundred percent escape artists today were these two," Houdini said, putting his arms around the shoulders of Nathaniel and Ace. "Bess, we must postpone our trip to Atlantic City for at least one more day. Tomorrow evening, it will be our pleasure to perform a few incomparable mysteries —Metamorphosis, a handcuff escape, and perhaps some *playing card* illusions—for our colleague Ace, his family, and his invited friends."

"Honest?" asked Ace. "Can you come, Fuller, ah, Nate . . . and your mother?"

"I would love to meet your family, Ace," Deborah Fuller said. "I am sure Nathan feels the same."

"Mr. Houdini, what is wrong with you?" Bess asked. "You seem unhappy suddenly."

"I am surprised, my wily Wilhelmina. Customarily, when I suggest doing card tricks, you repeat the saying you have repeated for years. You should say: 'Mrs. Houdini knows that the straightest line to poverty is Mr. Houdini playing with cards—onstage or in a friendly game of poker.' But not tonight. Why?"

"I think that the audience tomorrow will be so special that you will be spectacular. I look forward to you doing card tricks for our new friends."

"Will wonders never cease?"

I doubt they ever do, Nate thought, *not when these people are involved.*

AUTHOR'S NOTE

Nathaniel Greene Makeworthy Fuller IV and his family are fictional characters, the invention of the author. But the danger they faced was very real.

From the 1850s to the present, unscrupulous criminals have deceived untold numbers of people in this country and around the world by faking contact with the dearly departed. Some were petty thieves, taking a dollar or two at a time. Others, like the fictional Mr. Trane, worked elaborate confidence games and netted fortunes. Tragically, a number of phony mediums really did commit murders for profit. Although many mediums, past and present, have been sincere people who firmly believe in their clairvoyant abilities, too many have been heartless frauds.

Grieving, suggestible targets of crime like Aunt Alice needed protectors. Houdini was their champion. The renowned escape artist and magician spent an enormous amount of his time and money unmasking fraudulent mediums. He crisscrossed the country giving lectures that illustrated the tricks criminals used. He employed a team of private investigators to ferret out crooked mediums and alert local police to their activities. Houdini often disguised himself through wigs, beards, and false noses so he could secretly attend séances and expose the shams himself.

Nearly all of the statements Houdini makes in this book regarding mediums and his personal beliefs are quoted from Houdini's books, magazine articles, and statements made to the press.

Houdini's home at 278 West 113th Street is faithfully described, but not in as great detail as it deserves. The huge brownstone was bursting with oddities that Houdini collected.

In 1911, the city of New York—always in transition—was experiencing dramatic population growth and the introduction of new technologies that radically changed the urban lifestyle. The city is depicted as factually as this work of fiction permitted. A real Nate Fuller could have lived in a private house on East Fifty-third Street and clerked at a hatmaker's on lower Fifth Avenue. But he could not have worked at Bennett & Son, because it never existed. Neither did the City Hotel, where Nate was held prisoner. Similarly, Houdini escaped from a rattan hamper just as described, but not at Keith's 125th Street Theater.

Those switches from the absolutely true to the partially true are generally described as artistic license. Think of it as a fudge factor that helps an author tell the best story possible.

TOM LALICKI

What sparked your interest in Harry Houdini? Why did you decide to develop a mystery series around Houdini?

My first recognition of Houdini as an iconic figure came from reading *Ragtime*. The portrait of Houdini in E. L. Doctorow's turn-of-the-previous-century social-history novel made it clear that Houdini's stature as a public figure was enormous.

As I researched his life for a biography called *Spellbinder*, it became clear that Houdini was an A+ celebrity before the A-List was invented. Many people have been called the "Most Famous Person of the first-half of the 20th Century": Louis Armstrong, Shirley Temple, Charlie Chaplin, Babe Ruth, Winston Churchill. But it's Houdini who constantly appears in popular fiction and film. It's Houdini who entered the dictionary as a verb: "to do a Houdini." It's rare for a week to pass without my seeing his name in a newspaper or magazine. Houdini has a hold on the popular psyche unsurpassed by any of his contemporaries. Houdini is on a plateau with Elizabeth I, another frequent subject of films, novels, and biographies. People just can't get enough of either of them.

Even so, while everyone knows the name Houdini, very few know anything about the real Houdini. Most of the lore made popular by films is outrageously false. Houdini did not die attempting a trick too difficult to perform as depicted in a film starring Tony Curtis. Nor did he come to believe in fairy photography as a recent movie contended. In fact, Houdini unmasked numerous fairy- and spirit-photography hoaxes and never found a single one to be genuine.

My research for *Spellbinder* revealed many intriguing but obscure facets of a man who aspired to be more than an entertainer. Houdini was a lifelong student of the history of magic and related arts. He was a generous and anonymous philanthropist. He performed countless free shows for disabled children in hospitals, for institutionalized orphans, and for prison inmates. He was a man of boundless enthusiasm and energy. In 1926, the year of his death, Houdini was deeply involved in researching an encyclopedia of superstition, creating a curriculum for a University of Magic he planned to open, preparing to enroll at Columbia University as an undergraduate, and lecturing against the criminal abuse of phony mediums.

The impetus for writing *Danger in the Dark* was, in fact, Houdini's anguish over the plight of people duped by spiritualists. Houdini was sickened by the harm done to vulnerable people. Their hopes were abused, their money was stolen, their spirits were wrecked. History records numerous suicides and murders that stemmed from manipulation by mediums. But Houdini didn't wring his hands and moan about it. He employed a team of roving private detectives to root out fraudulent mediums and turn them over to the police. He turned down profitable bookings to do informational lecture tours that lost him money. And, yes, he adopted all sorts of disguises and attended the séances of particularly sophisticated mediums to see if they were frauds.

More stories just flow from Houdini's life. He knew a tremendous amount about crime and freely offered his advice to police. One prominent chief of police was only half-joking when he said "Thank heavens that Houdini's honest. If he wasn't, we'd have had to kill him years ago."

Teaming up with a famous person is a fantasy many of us would like to experience—how did you develop this concept?
Harry and Bess Houdini deeply regretted that they were unable to have children of their own. They could have adopted a child, but I can only guess they did not because customs were different a century ago. Nonetheless, they were in the presence of children and young adults a great deal. Houdini loved performing for children, especially orphans and hospitalized children. Houdini and his wife shared the misfortune of losing their fathers early in life. Houdini especially grieved for the father he lost too early.

I asked myself "what would happen if an inquisitive but sheltered boy who never had a father came into their lives. And how would they react when they discovered that boy was facing a life-threatening situation only Houdini could unravel?" After determining who that surrogate son was—Nathaniel Greene Makeworthy Fuller IV—the story fell into place. (Because Houdini had done—and written about—much of the action in my story.)

The Houdini & Nate books are set in the past, but are exciting and accessible to today's readers. Why do you think this is so?
The way people lived in the past, the resources and technology they had available, and the belief systems they valued and lived by were very different. To me, it's critical to try to represent people the way they really were. At the same time, human motivation never changes. Pride, envy, greed, and the rest could be called the eternal motivators rather than deadly sins. *Our* basic needs—food, shelter, companionship—are the same today as they were for our pre-linguistic Adams and Eves a half million years ago. What changes is the context in which we try to attain our needs—and wants.

The challenge of historical fiction is to understand the time you are writing about well enough to make the characters true to their time and understandable to the reader today.

**This is your first work of fiction. Did writing
Danger in the Dark differ from how you wrote
your previous nonfiction books?**

For good or bad, my approach is the same. While writing *Danger in the Dark*, I filled up a three-inch, three-ring binder with hundreds of pages of research material.

W. W. Brands, a great living historian, once pointed out that if you want to be famous forever, start keeping a diary today. Don't fill it with your thoughts about politics or international affairs—there are thousands of others writing about that. Instead, just describe what you ate today, what kind of clothes you wore, what your trip to school was like. Keep your diaries in a safe place all your life; then donate them to a university library. A hundred years later, when historians have no idea how we lived day-to-day, they will call your diaries invaluable and quote you in their books for generations to come.

That's a long way of saying that the most difficult thing about writing historical fiction is accurately describing how characters lived their lives every day. I found myself repeatedly asking questions like: "What kind of taxi would Nate take? Would it be horse-drawn or an automobile? When did fingerprints become available? Where did you get the Staten Island Ferry in 1911 and what did Staten Island look like when you got off the ferry?"

Then you get into really difficult daily living questions like: "What does a slate pencil used on a slate board look like, since they did not use chalk then?" or "If Nate bought a notebook to use as a journal, what would the notebook have looked like? Did notebooks exist then? Or composition books?"

You can see how three-ring binders are easily filled answering questions like that. Of course, doing research you discover unexpected and fascinating things about the past, like what the first "rubberneckers" did and how to properly eat a banana.

In writing history and biography, an author has a historical record. There are always indisputable facts that form the core of a biography. Of course, those facts are always subject to interpretation. For example, it is fair to say "George Washington crossed the ice-bound Delaware River with his troops because he thought the American Revolution would collapse unless he roused patriotic fervor by winning a battle." It is fair to say that because his writings and the recollections of people with whom he spoke support that contention. It is not fair to say "While standing in the boat Washington probably thought 'This will make me a real hero' or 'I wish I had stayed home in Mount Vernon instead' or 'Crap, this coat has a big gravy stain on it.'"

In non-fiction and biography, I believe it is unprofessional and deceptive to ascribe thoughts or feelings or motives to real people that are not supported by fact. On the other hand, that is precisely what writing fiction is all about. And truthfully, I was surprised to discover that the more you write about fictional characters, the more aggressive they become about what they say and how they feel.

As characters blossom on the page—developing distinct personalities, having idiosyncratic behaviors—they become very real. So real that they often wake me up in the middle of the night to suggest "I would do this, not that, on page 48." Another will complain that "I wouldn't be caught dead saying or doing or wearing such and such."

When writing fiction, it pays to have paper and pen on your night table, so you're ready to take dictation from your characters.

In answer to answer some of our usual questions:

My best, and favorite, subject in school was history. A trait I share with Nate is that my worst subject always was and always shall be math.

My first job was working nights and weekends in an unheated ice-cream stand open ten months a year in upstate New York. Every job after that was easier in retrospect.

I used to write in my office, but an orthopedic affliction sentenced me to bed while writing *Shots at Sea*. Now it's entirely natural to work with a Mac laptop on my knee.

When I finish a book, my editor reads it. But long before finishing a manuscript I bounce chapters, ideas, paragraphs, everything, in fact, off my most trusted reader, Barbara Lalicki—my best friend and most gifted critic for (gasp) nearly forty years.

My idea of a best meal is sampling everything on the buffet of a really good Indian restaurant. The single most perfect such meal I remember eating was in a family-owned Bengali restaurant in Prague that looked out upon the ancient Jewish cemetery that Barbara and I had spent hours touring.

I have more than 14,000 album cuts on my iPods, so singling out a favorite song isn't feasible. A favorite artist? At least one, if not more than one, of the many creative incarnations of Miles Davis.

I will enthusiastically admit that John Dortmunder is my favorite fictional character, that *The Big Bang Theory* is my favorite TV show, and that if I could go anywhere in time I would like to be with that small, extended-family group of humans who first recognized that they could communicate more than hunger, anger, and desire by using sounds. Think of what it must have been like to actually go around naming animals and plants and even relatives.

What I would most like readers to remember about my books is enjoying them.
And, I'd like to share the best writing advice I ever got. I had this cellotaped to my monitor while writing *Danger in the Dark*. It's from an interview with E. L. Doctorow: "Writing a novel is like driving a car at night. You can only see as far as your headlights, but you can make the whole trip that way."

Nate and Houdini think they're sailing to England for a nice rest after their last harrowing adventure, but they're in for a big surprise when they find out an assassin is aboard their ship.

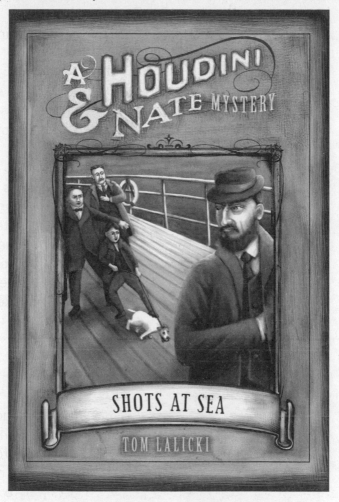

Keep reading for an excerpt from

Shots at Sea

by Tom Lalicki

Prologue

An *idler standing about, day after day, watching other peo-ple work. That's Aunt Alice's definition of a loafer,* Nate thought. *A pleasure hound.* The idea troubled Nate but didn't prevent him from walking south to Fourteenth Street and west to the Hudson River three mornings in a row. By the time he reached Pier 54, there were always dozens of people already gathered.

Many were street vendors, ready to sell the hungry sea-men sandwiches, fruit, even ice cream. Boys with empty growlers were poised to fetch beer in the metal pails from local taverns for a tip. Nate assumed the crowd included a fair number of pickpockets and confidence men looking for an easy buck. He kept an eye peeled, hoping to catch one in action.

But most of the crowd just gaped and gawked—for good reason. It took colossal amounts of supplies and human toil to ready the world's largest ship for a crossing from New York to England. Nate had seen the end of the coaling. Twenty-two trains of coal—nearly twelve million pounds—had been unloaded and shoveled belowdecks by hand. To remove the thick, black film of dust left behind, the deck crew hosed and wiped down the entire ship before food could be loaded. Nate counted as one hundred and thirty pigs and one hundred and fifty sheep and lambs were hauled onboard. He stopped counting turkeys, ducks, geese, and pigeons when he overheard a fellow spectator say that the *Lusitania* always stocked over five thousand different fowl in its kitchen.

How many of these people will board with us tomorrow? Nate wondered as he slowly surveyed the crowd. Sizing people up one at a time, he assigned everyone to either the "sailing" or the "not sailing" category. And for each person judged to be sailing, Nate fixed upon a characteristic—a style of dress, a way of standing or walking, a unique facial feature—that would help him identify the person during the voyage.

I'll write to Houdini, if I get enough right.

Nate had met the world's most famous illusionist and his wife by sheer chance—which had proved very lucky for him, his mother, and especially his great-aunt Alice.

She had fallen for the lies of a swindler who intended to take her money and, quite probably, her life, too. But Houdini had teamed up with Nate to expose the criminal's scheme and imprison his gang. In the process, Houdini had taken a shine to the boy because of Nate's powers of observation and his pluck, but they hadn't seen each other for months as the Houdinis toured the country.

Nate made his notes about the people he watched in the red leather-bound journal he had bought to record his thoughts and observations. After all, accurate note-taking skills were essential for any detective. When people didn't fit into either of his original categories, he called them "maybes."

One "maybe" caught his eye because the man was so unusual—eccentric, even. Nate described him as "Tall, young, thin with thinning hair. Walk undistinguished. Circular purple birthmark (wart?) on left nostril." Nate underlined the last sentence, thinking that the man would be easy to recognize with that purple splotch. He looked at "Maybe #3" again.

"Very agitated—always in motion. Wears overcoat (no hat!) even though warm and sunny for October."

How could Nate have known that the man with the purple splotch on his nose and the unnecessary overcoat was concealing a Smith & Wesson New Century revolver? The gun had a four-inch barrel and was loaded with .44-caliber cartridges. A close-range shot to the head or body would invariably kill its target.

Unfamiliar with guns, the man in the overcoat was getting used to the feel of carrying a weapon. He feared that using it was another matter entirely.

The agitated man had test-fired the revolver dozens of times without bullets, but he knew that calmly walking up, leveling the barrel, and firing into the chest of a living human being was . . . terrifying. Terrifying and exciting. *It's my job—my duty,* the man told himself over and over again as he paced around the pier.

Screwing up his courage, the man in the overcoat told himself he *would* board the ship. He *would* track down his prey and execute him. He *would* strike a blow for liberty! For a better, brighter future!

How could Nate have guessed any of it, eager as he was to begin his first great ocean-voyage adventure?

1

Standing at the foot of the gangplank, Nate finally believed they were going. He had made a dozen trips to the tailor, accompanied his mother on numberless shopping excursions for travel necessities, and endured three bon voyage dinners with his aunt's elderly friends. He had even sent a note to Ace Winchell, his onetime partner in crime fighting.

Suitcases, trunks, and hatboxes with enough clothes for his mother and great-aunt Alice—a whole year's worth—were already stowed in the first-class cabin Nate would share with them. At this point, they simply had to climb the narrow, steeply angled wooden gangplank—the first-class gangplank—and follow a ship's steward to their cabin.

But Nate had learned enough about life—the hard way—to value a warning Houdini had given him: "We can never really tell what is ever likely to happen." Nate had climbed only a few steps when he heard his great-aunt's voice below.

"I should not be here, Deborah," she told her niece-in-law, Nate's mother.

"We should go to our cabin. You will feel much better when we settle in," Deborah Fuller replied.

"That is not true. I am far too old for foolishness like this." Aunt Alice shook her head dramatically. "I should never have allowed myself to be bullied and badgered."

"It's just last-minute nerves, Aunt Alice. I have them myself."

"It is not nerves, Deborah, it is clear thinking," Aunt Alice insisted. Nate's mother sighed slightly, searching for the right thing to say.

"Pardon me, ladies," a portly, well-dressed man standing behind them said. "May I be of assistance? If you need help boarding, I will gladly go first and send a steward to aid you."

"I do not need a steward, sir. I need to return to my own home," Aunt Alice said decisively.

"Aunt Alice, let's step aside and let others board while we discuss this," Deborah suggested. "Nate, go ahead and send a steward to us."

"In a flash," Nate said, turning and climbing the gang-plank quickly enough to escape his aunt's protests. Touching foot onboard the enormous ship made him quiver with anticipation. He was incredibly eager to explore the length and breadth of every deck of the enormous vessel, but a uniformed officer purposefully blocked his path.

"Your name, sir?" the officer asked in a polite, accented voice. The ship was owned and mostly staffed by Britons.

"Nathaniel Fuller. I am traveling with my mother, Deborah Fuller, and my great-aunt."

The officer flipped through the papers on his clipboard. "And your great-aunt's name is . . . ?"

"Mrs. Ludlow, Mrs. Alice Ludlow."

"Yes, I have the Ludlow-Fuller party in B-6, a three-person saloon-class accommodation on B-deck forward . . ."

"I thought that we were in first class," Nate said. "My aunt can't bear the *thought* of saloons. She certainly isn't going to sleep near one."

"And she will not, my young American gentleman," said the British officer, choking back a laugh. "Our saloon class is the height of luxury, far exceeding your expectation of first class."

"So saloon class doesn't mean saloon, it means first?" Nate asked. "Why not call it first class?"

"Some people think that Americans and British are one people separated by the sharing of a common language," the officer said, as if that answered Nate's question. "But are those two ladies standing by the side of the gangplank your mother and aunt? Why haven't they boarded yet?"

"My aunt is . . . reconsidering the trip."

"A bit late in the day for that, wouldn't you say? Let's go down and sort things out."

"I don't think my going is the best idea. I could never convince my aunt to do anything. Certainly not to change her mind. But I don't think she will let me sail to England by myself."

"I'd take a flyer on that," the officer said, winking for emphasis. Nate was unsure what precisely "taking a flyer" was, but translation could wait.

"You said we are in Cabin B-6?"

"Yes, quite a spacious forward cabin. It's toward the bow on the starboard side—that is the right side, you know—of B-deck," the officer said.

"And *port* is left and the rear is the *stern*," Nate said.

"Jolly good. Now, when I return with your mother and aunt, this steward will guide you."

"No need for that. I can find it myself, after I attend to some business." Nate hotfooted it away, happy to let a stranger lock wills with his great-aunt.

"Business!" an eavesdropping steward whispered skeptically to himself. "The bairn's hardly old enough for long pants. Business indeed!"